FOR THE SAKE OF IT

Copyright © 2022 by Ekjoatroop
Bikramī 2078
Nanakshāhī 553

All rights reserved. No part of this book may be reproduced or transmitted in any form or by any means without written permission from the publisher.

ISBN 978-1-8381437-5-6
KhalisHouse Publishing

www.KhalisHouse.com
info@KhalisHouse.com

Find us on:
Instagram/KhalisHouse
Twitter/KhalisHouse

Khalis House
Publishing
Read today. Lead tomorrow.

With the Blessings of Waheguru

For those who came before
Who strived to lay the foundation for the youth of today
And gave everything so we could have a chance to
thrive

Thank you,
To my family, peers, and mentors
KS, MI, and MO Sangat
Rajnarind Kaur
Jeannette Bonjour
Harbaldeep Singh
Jasvir Kaur Singh

ACKNOWLEDGEMENTS

My original inspiration for the novel was stemmed in the idea of equality, humanity, and revealing the truth behind discrimination and power. I wrote the story because I thought it could offer a new perspective. I wanted to bring the change I believe is overdue. We are not where we were ten years ago and I hope the next ten will bring more understanding and empathy but while the world is changing, many people are refusing change with it. It is the very stubbornness of human nature that causes this, I suppose, but there is no excuse for the seething hatred that rages through many corners of the world. I was able to get the story and its themes together, but I could not have come this far without the help and support of the people around me.

I want to thank my mom and sister for listening to me work out the details of my story for well over hours on end. I want to thank my younger brothers for being straightforward about the ideas I often presented in front of them and thank my dad for pushing me to release the book even if I felt that it would never be ready.

Thank you Rajnarind Aunty, for reading through the first few drafts of the story and giving me thoughtful and honest feedback. Your support and encouragement made this possible. I truly could not have done it without you!

And Jasvir Aunty, who offered another perspective with a more literary approach to details and the overall plot, thank you for taking your time out to help me.

Thank you Ms. Bonjour for giving me the opportunity to first put my work out for others to read and often helping me revise my own stories. It gave me the courage to even consider approaching a project of this size. Truly, thank you.

And to my publisher, Ranveer Singh, thank you for working with me to iron out the odds and ends of the novel, so that it could get ready to be published.

To Harbaldeep Uncle (Founder & Mentor, Nishkam TV) and my peers and mentors from SALDEF, thank you for encouraging me to become much more than what I believed was possible.

Lastly, thank you to KS, MI, and MO sangat who have supported me ever since I first performed Kirtan. Your blessings stay with me, always.

PROLOGUE

The Aftermath of the Third World War

The Senate office was lined with crimson wallpaper and old wood, but the curtains remained closed despite the midday sun. Its seat, this cold morning, was occupied by a new man. General Griffin had made a name for himself, and still in his prime, his conquests had left him with high prospects. Power, money, and reputation. He had everything, and despite the outcome of a failed war that weighed heavy on the hearts of Americans, his power seemed to have grown to new heights.

A muffled knock disrupted the silence, and the general, previously lost in his thoughts, returned to the world again.

"Come in," he said roughly.

A young man in his twenties entered curiously.

"You wanted to see me, Andrew?" The general granted the man permission to sit with nothing more than the wave of a hand. They had fought in the war together, side by side, and while he acknowledged that the man was as clever as he was intelligent, the matter at hand was too serious to dismiss.

"Lieutenant Singh." General Griffin tilted his head and looked over at the man he formerly believed to be a friend. "You must be ecstatic," he said with a smile. It was wide and far too joyous to be his, but it was nothing more than an afterthought. General Griffin's eyes were what had caught the lieutenant's attention. They were hysterical and filled

1

with unbound chaos that seemed to bring him to the edge of insanity.

"Why, Sir?"

"With the outcome of the war, of course!" the general explained. "Your people won." He laughed, and the sight was nothing less than unusual.

"We lost, Sir. America lost."

"Yes, I'm aware, but your people won." Lieutenant Singh watched carefully as General Griffin rose from his seat to approach him. He stood as well, but his eyes never left those of his comrade's. The general glanced at the man's dark dastaar with disgust.

"What are you? Turkish? Pakistani?"

"American," he answered calmly. The general grabbed the man's collar.

"What are you," he asked slowly. Lieutenant Singh's jaw ticked, but he did nothing more than read the situation. Surely, Andrew was still grappling with the embarrassment of his loss, of their loss. Surely, this was nothing more than a brief display of grief. Surely, he reasoned, this was not the man he had nearly died protecting.

"Panjabi," Lieutenant Singh replied.

General Griffin let go, and with it, the tension in the air dispelled.

"I expect your letter of resignation on my desk by tomorrow."

"Resignation, Sir? Why?"

The general returned to his seat, and again, he smiled. "You're one of them. It's the only reason we lost."

2

"Sir—"

"You and every other colored fool in this country!" Finally, his facade had fallen. "You came here and polluted this once prosperous nation. How else could we have lost, and to countries as barbaric as Nigeria and Panjab and Korea!"

"I was born here, Sir, raised here. This is my country."

The general shook his head in abhorrence.

"No, this is *my* country."

General Griffin's views spread across the nation in a matter of months, and by the next election, they had poisoned the minds of enough angry Americans to distort the votes in favor of a man who would later go on to become sovereign. The Constitution was rewritten and returned to its barest form as the Charter of Veracious, and over a decade later, America was unrecognizable.

Twenty Years Later, Present Day

CHAPTER ONE

Blood and Water

The chill of the cell had seeped into my bones by morning, but the sun's early rays washed over the rough concrete, warming my cold skin. The quiet was nothing short of peaceful, and the very air of this place seemed to change in the hours before his arrival. I could breathe in the mornings. They were one of the few things that hadn't changed in a world that I could no longer recognize as my own. The mornings were beautiful, bringing with them memories of what had been, so the reality of what was, started to seem a little farther away.

The cell door opened with a familiar creak, and with the sound came an unusual feeling. My hand would start twitching, and my heart began to beat a little faster, but the amiable light kept the actions at bay. Night had passed, and so another day had dawned. There was little to worry about until the work began, and as long as I behaved how I had learned to, I would be fine. But then again, I rarely worried for myself. The pain had grown to be somewhat of a second skin, and the scars, the bruises, I had learned to wear as medals. They were a testament to who I was and what I refused to become. Still, they did not bring with them the comfort I often found myself longing for. The warmth of family, the forgotten life I had once had, and the freedom I had left behind.

The Overseer walked through the cell door and crouched down in front of me.

"You attacked one of my men." I had, but the reason behind the violence meant nothing in a place like this. To him, my argument was as baseless as my name, and my word was as meaningless as his.

"Let's see if I can finally break you." He grabbed me by my shirt collar and pushed me into the cold, grey wall hard enough to bruise my chained hands. His salt and pepper hair fell over his angry blue eyes, but it was not an emotion that I had caused. Regardless, I paid for its consequences.

He drove his fist into my abdomen, and the air left my lungs. My temple grazed the hard concrete when his knuckles connected with my jaw, then my cheekbone, before he threw me onto the floor. My shoulder took the brunt of the force, and my nose grazed the dust for just a second before I pushed myself up.

The action made him angrier.

I didn't fight back. I took it because I had to, because fighting made it worse. I took it because they worried when I came back like I had the last time, but I took the liberty to maintain my silence. I didn't cry out. I didn't apologize for something I had no reason to regret. Many had come to label the defiance as an act of pride, but it was more than that. It was a silent declaration that I still had the self-respect he wished to take from me and that despite the circumstances, I had managed to hold onto my dignity.

"Sir." He let go and turned to the guard who had dared to interrupt him, his breathing heavy and uneven.

"He's here."

The Overseer's breath caught in his throat before he stepped away. His bloody hands dusted off his bright white shirt, and the crimson that smeared on the cloth imprinted on it a message that was still unspoken by the inhabitants of this dark place. It was a tribute to those still ignorant of the truth and witness to the wrath of a man no longer human.

He left without a word.

I didn't move from my place in the cell until a guard came to take me back to the cabins. He pushed me forward and cursed when my blood covered the tips of his fingers, but he didn't otherwise act, and that was a blessing all on its own.

The sun blanketed my skin, and the wind, the heavenly wind, was gentle as it blew past to rid me of the cold that had previously clung to me like honey. Spring had come, and with it, a promise of something new. Life was no longer held captive by winter, and the flowers had finally begun to bloom.

I opened the wooden door and walked in with my head hung low. The others had probably started their work in the fields, so the cabin would be empty, I thought, but it was not. The stillness was broken by the echo of rushed footsteps. I raised my eyes and smiled when they met with those of a friend's, a sister's. She grabbed my arm and brushed her light fingers over my jaw, only letting go when I flinched at the sudden pain. She wiped away the stray tear that had fallen from her chocolate brown eyes and I stayed quiet as she pulled me inside.

"Let's get you cleaned up." Naina led me to a corner of the cabin, and we sat down.

"The Overseer gave us the day off," she said with a small smile. I matched hers with one of my own, though mine was only moderately forced.

"Where are the others?" She twisted the water out of an old cloth and cleaned the blood off my skin. It gave her solace to take care of me, and the thought was enough to keep me still.

"Dalmar wanted to talk to Amrit, and Ali hasn't come back yet."

"Is everything alright?" Her smile remained, but the light in her eyes faded.

"Is anything ever?" I laughed lightly before my eyes settled on the floor.

"The Overseer has a guest." The cloth dropped from her hands.

"Is it—"

"No. He was joyful, and there was no intimidation. I don't know who it could be." She ran a hand through her short dark hair as the door opened once more. A youthful man walked through it and approached us.

"How are you?" Amrit's eyes crinkled at the corners like they often did when he worried.

I shrugged in response.

"Good, Veere." He smiled at the word that marked him as my brother but frowned at the sight of my bruises.

"He didn't hold back, did he?" he asked softly as he sat down. I offered a smile to comfort him, and along with it, a small laugh.

"It was nothing I couldn't handle."

"What did Dalmar want to talk about?" Naina asked.

"The Overseer's son is coming today, so we can't leave the cabins until nightfall. I don't think they want us interfering with what they have planned."

"Should we be worried?" He sighed, wary.

"I don't know."

Those words had defined so much of my recent existence, and too much had been left to uncertainty. I didn't know what we had done to have been sent here or if this was because of any fault of our own. I didn't know if there would be a reason to laugh tomorrow, and truthfully, I didn't even know if we would make it another day. I had learned to survive, but I was often left wondering how long we would. It was a lingering thought that said enough on its own.

We had forgotten how to live.

Ever since Independence Day a few years ago, nothing had been the same. I suppose we should have seen it coming, but I was too naive to believe that the nation could do something so cruel. Perhaps it was a consequence of youth to believe in something as irrational and ambitious as humanity.

We paid no heed to the door as it opened and closed until the last member of our makeshift family had returned. Ali walked into the cabin and sat down by my brother, his lopsided smile as bright as ever, though I hardly noticed it. My eyes studied the dark spots of color that littered his skin.

"When did you get those bruises?" It was an innocent question that held more weight to me now than it had ever before. He glanced down at them, and Naina did what she could to hide hers.

He smiled faintly at my concern. He was as much a brother to me as Amrit, and even though we didn't share blood, I had grown up with him, so he was family.

"After they took you last night, they made a handful of us stay past sunset to finish up the work. They were drunk," he said, "and really angry."

I nodded and leaned onto the cabin wall for support. It hurt to breathe, and it was hard to move, but I barely noticed my own wounds.

"Do they hurt?"

"No," she said.

I didn't believe her. I would take a beating for them, even lay down my life for the chance that even one of them could make it out of here to find something better. Their wounds hurt more than my own, and it was a type of pain that didn't heal quickly.

The atmosphere changed with a smile.

"Do you remember the first time I tried to ride a bike?" Naina asked, eager to change the subject. I thought back.

"You scraped your knee."

9

"And we fought for the first time because I was so upset." Ali said as he rubbed his eyes to hide his embarrassment. Naina laughed.

"It was justified!" he defended.

"She was five, Ali," my brother countered.

"I told you to wait for me to help you."

"It was my first bike. I was excited!" Naina replied.

"You ran into a tree!"

She gave him a big cheeky smile and ruffled his dark hair. It fell over his ocean eyes as they lit up. He pushed her hand away but didn't bother to fix it. There was no point.

"We had to go to your house and apologize." I laughed softly at the memory. It was a blessing to reminisce.

"Yeah," he said with a smile. "The chocolate really won me over." Naina let out a dramatic sigh as she fell back.

"What I would do for chocolate right now. I'd even take that weird dark chocolate that tastes like black coffee on steroids."

"Ammi loved dark chocolate. She would always have a piece after dinner." He paused. "I wonder if she's eaten today." Ali's distant voice was enough to shatter whatever joy had come with the beautiful nostalgia of old memories.

My smile fell at his words, and tears filled my eyes at the mention of his mother. It reminded me of my own.

"I'm sure they're fine," Amrit's voice broke near the end.

"Can we ..."

"Yeah."

We sat down facing each other as we prayed together. It gave me a sense of relief to know that wherever they were, they prayed under the same sun, and the moon lit the same land they stood on. My family had someone looking out for them when I couldn't, and there was nothing more I could ask for.

Three Weeks Before Independence Day

CHAPTER TWO

A Friendship Deeper Than Blood

"Give it back!" I shot forward and stumbled into the kitchen counter, the ache that came from the contact unexpected, but momentary. It did nothing to deter me from my goal, to get back the book my brother had so slyly taken from me. Amrit glanced back with a laugh.

"Veere, I'm warning you." I could practically hear my heart beating in my ears as I glared at him. The smile that had disappeared, if only for a second, crept back slowly in response to my words. Mischief glinted in his eyes, and I knew that my warning had gone unheeded.

"Veere—"

"Kids! We're home!"

His smile disappeared as I made a move for the door. He had only just gotten back from university because of Thanksgiving break, but it wouldn't matter to our parents. Circumstance would change nothing. He would always be their only son and their oldest child. For me, that meant that I would get away with more than he ever could. This was just one of those things.

"Papa—"

"Welcome back!" Amrit jumped in front of me before I could finish. He hid the book behind him and offered it back to me discreetly. I took it with a quiet sigh.

My parents looked between us with curious expressions. Mama was the first to laugh as she closed the door.

"You two look like you had fun."

"You didn't get into another fight, now did you?"

"No," Amrit was quick to answer, but Papa didn't look at him. His eyes were on me.

I'm not sure what he expected. I would respond how I always did because even when I was too angry to look Amrit in the eye, I never had the heart to betray our bond, our friendship, so I never told Papa about our small quarrels. And even though I was usually on the receiving end of his pranks, I knew they meant as much as the words exchanged in the heat of our arguments. As was my relationship with my brother, unwavering, however tested. I shook my head and changed the topic of conversation.

"How was work?" Amrit hung Papa's coat, and I took his briefcase, the only communication between us his usual smile. It was Papa's way of saying thank you after a long day.

"Uneventful."

He made the short journey to the kitchen, and I was left alone again with my brother. He slung his arm over my shoulder, and I looked at him calmly. It never ceased to surprise me how much he had grown ever since he had left. His eyes were duller like they had seen more of the pain that resided outside the walls of my home. Maybe they had, or maybe he had finally started to grow up in a world that had already torn apart his childhood. Of course, I still had yet to grow out of mine.

"You know I love you."

I wanted to laugh, but instead, I turned to stare at a random photograph on the wall that pictured the entire family. We had managed to find matching blue dastaars for all of us, and it was the only picture we had taken in the past few years. The action was enough to divert his attention away from me, and that was all I needed to get my sweet revenge. I slammed my foot onto his toes as hard as I could before running towards the kitchen. He couldn't catch me, and he was too proud to admit his pain, so he put on a calm facade as he stood next to me by the counter. There was only one thing I could say.

"I love you too."

It was a whisper in the air, but it reached his ears and earned me a smile. He had forgiven me just as I had forgiven him. I could do nothing but remember a moment as delicate and precious as this one and hope that one day, I could find something similar if I could ever be free of my chains. These memories were insignificant in the order of things, but they were the only ones I seemed to remember. All that didn't matter, and everything I was too young to understand, I thought of now. I suppose it was the nature of life to remember and repent and to hope for the possibility to live through it again.

I slipped away to my room as the three began to talk. It was tranquil and the only place in the house filled with anything but sound and motion. It was my own space, and I had chosen to keep it simple. I put the novel on top of my stack of books before returning to my family.

We had just begun to make dinner when the phone rang, so Papa left to answer it. I didn't think much of it then, but looking back, it seemed unusual to get a call so late at night. Sure, the sun had only fallen an hour or two ago, but the sound was a variance in a world filled with regularity. Mama and Papa needed the phone for work, but it fell silent in the evenings. The outside world didn't disturb us then, and it was peaceful for a few hours. The ringing itself should have been enough to call for my attention, but I didn't mind it. I must have been too naive to worry. Papa returned and put the phone in my hand.

"It's for you." That was all he said before he turned away to help my mother. I stepped out of the kitchen, curious as the noise returned.

"Hello?"

"I ... I—" The voice on the other side trembled, nearly to the point of tears, and my heart stopped for a moment.

"Ali? Where are you?" He didn't answer as Amrit slipped out of the kitchen a few feet away from me. His expression was filled with interest, though his smile disappeared when he saw my pale face in the dim lights of the hallway.

"Is everything okay?" Amrit asked. I shook my head, too occupied with Ali's danger to consider his words.

"Where are you?" I repeated.

"Twenty-Third Street." There was relief in his answer, but the worry that came with it was greater than before. He was in the bad part of the city.

"I'm coming."

It only took me a moment to collect myself before I told my brother.

"We need to go now, Veere. You didn't hear him. I think he's hurt, really hurt." I pushed through the uncertainty and replaced it with the knowledge that time was limited.

"He'll be OK," he assured. An unusual seriousness had replaced Amrit's otherwise jovial manner as I followed him to the door and slipped on my coat.

"Where are you two off to?" My mother's voice was stern and incredibly terrifying. I looked to my brother for an answer, my eyes wide and my mouth too dry to speak.

"W-We're going to meet the others."

Mama's expression didn't change, but Papa couldn't help watching us with a small grin.

"They're just kids. Let them go, dear," he said, his tone lighter than usual.

"It's the middle of the night," she argued.

"Your mother's right." Papa sighed. His expression fell before it returned.

"Be back before ten."

There was only a second to move before my mother retaliated, and it was in that second that Amrit grabbed my arm and pulled me outside. The humor had long since faded as we walked in the cold with our thoughts, and the silence hung firmly between us until I decided to voice mine.

"Why didn't you tell them?"

He glanced at me before looking away. "They're exhausted." The extra hours had not been kind to my parents, and the people who worked above them didn't seem to care about anything but profit, but it was good work, and it paid well, so they never complained.

"We should have told them. You know I don't like keeping things from them."

"You can tell them after we come back."

"They might be able to help, you know. We could have actually taken the car instead of walking." Naina and Ali only lived a few feet away, so asking for the keys would have been unusual.

Amrit was quiet for a moment before he responded.

"I don't want them to get hurt."

I looked away, dejected. He was a protector, my brother. He always had been. It was his biggest weakness and his greatest strength.

His smile returned, though his tone remained somber as he continued, "You shouldn't be here either, you know. The fewer people, the better."

I tried to suppress my smile. "Then I think I should apologize."

"For what?"

I ran back the few steps it took to get to Naina's house before he could grab my arm. We had just walked past her driveway, so it was viable for me to get there before Amrit, an all-around athlete, caught up to me. I knocked on the door and pulled her outside as soon as she saw me.

"Ali's in trouble. We have to go."

I could hear my brother slam his palm to his forehead.

"What are you doing?" he whispered as Naina stepped inside to grab her coat.

"I'll get the bikes," she offered.

Amrit grew quiet after she ran off to grab the bicycles we had left here sometime this past summer.

"You could tell me next time."

I ignored his annoyance with a small smile. "I was trying to protect you."

"That doesn't even make sense!"

"Exactly! That's why we should tell them!"

"No." He was more serious than I had seen him in a long time.

I respected him enough to listen. It didn't matter if I thought he was wrong, and it was only because of one reason. I knew he would leave if I went back, and I didn't want him to do this alone. He was my brother, so I guess we would have to face the consequences together.

"Fine," I said quietly.

"Where to?" Naina asked. I opened the zipper to my coat as I got onto my faded blue bicycle.

"Twenty-Third Street."

We didn't stop until we turned into the row of shops marking the beginning of our destination. It was safer to stay together, and despite our short journey, I still worried that we had come too late.

It was hard to see in the darkness even with the shine of the streetlamps, so while the others squinted, I had resorted to listening, intently, for the hope that he would notice us before we found him.

I tensed at the small, distinct sound of a cough. I couldn't recognize it, but the hope was enough to push me towards the noise.

"Ali?"

He turned into the light of the lamps, and my breath caught in my throat. His face was filled with cuts and bruises, and his clothes, previously wrinkled, were soaked with blood. Naina ran towards him and helped Amrit as he put his arm around Ali's neck. I was left to make sure the street stayed as empty as it was. There were a few strangers rushing to get home and another few waiting in the shadows.

I would have worried, not for myself but Ali, had I been alone. I could handle myself well enough against someone else, but his condition meant that I had already lost before I began. I wasn't alone, though, so there was no more reason to worry. At least, I was naive enough to think so until Naina realized the time.

"We have three minutes until curfew." I could hear the sound of distant sirens and the occasional gunshot that rang far enough to reach my ears.

"What do we do?" Amrit asked.

"We can't leave him."

"No one's leaving anyone," I said. My hand pressed against the side of my head in an attempt to force a new idea. It never seemed to work, however. My thoughts always came of their own accord.

19

"The beach," Amrit offered. "We can make it if we hurry."

I snapped my fingers.

"There's a straight path from there to the park. It's discreet, so no one will see us."

"There's no time," Naina argued. "We're as good as dead if we step out there now."

Amrit turned to me. "What do we do?"

"Don't ask me!"

"You're the smart one! Come one, think, Meher!"

I looked out into the street, out into the darkness and the cover it gave the few souls who had decided to take the chance to go home. The beach was too far away, and this close to curfew, the police had already lined the exits. There was no way for us to return home without the risk of getting caught by people who were eager to use the guns that had grown too cold. There was really only one thing we could do.

"We wait."

"That's a death sentence," he countered. "His wounds-"

"They're better than they look." Naina's words were the only support I needed.

"I'm sure we'll be fine if we stay quiet."

Naina did what she could to help Ali as we crouched back into the darkness, and the night passed in the chaos that reigned outside the walls of my home.

I leaned into my brother, and he put his arm around me, ever the protector.

"Are you cold?"

"No."

"I can take the first watch, then. Get some sleep. I'll wake you up if anything happens."

He didn't wake me. He didn't have the strength to stay awake the entire night either, so it was anything but surprising when I woke up to the discomfort that came with the weight of his head on mine. I moved away and checked his wristwatch.

3:24 a.m.

Deep into the night, the natural silence had returned, and it was in this silence that I found an opportunity. I woke the others.

"If we leave now, we have a chance to get back before dawn."

"You woke me up for this?" Amrit groaned.

I hit him over the head. "Get it together, brother." My voice had refrained from the usual annoyance, and instead, it had adopted an underlying admiration. I had no way of knowing if we would make it out of here alive. This decision was another play with life and death, with survival and failure. It meant that their blood would be on my hands if I made a mistake. It would be my fault if anything happened to them, but it was my weight to bear. It was the first time in a long time that I had decided to do something alone. It was merely a decision, but it would be the first change of many.

"Let's go."

Twenty Days Before Independence Day

CHAPTER THREE

Consequences

The men tasked with upholding the integrity of curfew had long since fallen asleep, so we were able to slip out of the main part of the city without much trouble. The caution we had adopted kept us quiet and careful. Any movement out of turn, any sound out of place, would be the end of us. Our story had only just begun, but sometimes, when the world is too harsh for me to bear, I wonder if it would have been better if I had made a mistake and ended it right then and there.

The beach was unusually quiet that night. I rarely passed by it, but when I did, there were always a few friends laughing around a poorly made campfire or a couple walking by the ocean. It was always busy during the summer, but I suppose things had changed since I was a child.

Mama didn't want us going out anymore. Not that we did, originally, we had just taken to walking around the city when the weather permitted it. It was a different form of consolation for each of us. For me, it offered an empty time to perceive and wonder, to take in the world in its fundamental form and hope that it might change. I nearly laughed at my thoughts. I guess Ms. Garcia had rubbed off on me.

My eyes landed on the crashing waves as my pounding heart calmed. They drowned out the horrors of the silent city and brought in the peace that seemed increasingly rare as I grew older.

"Street fighting, Ali, of all things. What were you thinking?" Naina yelled quietly as she tended to Ali's wounds.

"He wasn't," I said as I turned away from the peace and reentered the life I had yet to truly live.

I sat down next to Naina and watched Amrit as he ripped the shirt under his jacket to make a usable bandage. The gash above Ali's eyebrow and the cuts under his torn shirt had stopped bleeding, but the bruises were only getting darker. A busted lip accompanied his black eye and bruised cheek, making him look more like the fighter he had pretended to be.

"How bad is he?" I asked. She sighed and glanced at me.

"He won't die from his wounds, that much I can tell you, but I can't say for certain that his parents won't kill him when they find out what he's been up to." Amrit sat down across from me as Ali opened his eyes. There was a small smile over his lips.

"You guys wouldn't let that happen," he replied, his voice rough and raw before he turned away to cough. I shrugged.

"I don't know if I'd give up my life for you." I leaned back against the rocks we had taken shelter behind as I mulled it over. "We would be on the run for the rest of our lives, or at least, as long as your parents are alive." Naina elbowed me, and I did my best to hide my smile.

"She's got a point," Amrit said, sighing. "You're on your own, man."

Ali's eyes grew frantic at the sight of our dismissal. He leaned forward and grabbed my brother by the arm.

"N-No, guys. You have to be there, or they might actually kill me."

Amrit pushed him back down with a smile.

"We've made it this far," he said with a laugh. "I guess we can see it through to the end."

We agreed with him, and it was an incredible mistake. The dread didn't set in until I realized it would take at least two hours to get back home. We were going to take the long way around to avoid getting caught, so we would get home late.

"What are we going to do?" I whispered to Amrit as we walked.

"What do you mean?"

"We left without telling Mama and Papa where we were going." He let out a tired sigh.

"Right."

"Forget about Ali; they're going to kill us too when they find out where we went." He shrugged in the darkness, still nonchalant.

"We'll be fine."

I was foolish enough to believe him.

The distant city clock rang six when we finally entered the safety of our neighborhood. I remember the dread settling in my bones and the stillness in the air. The wind had stopped blowing a while ago, and it did nothing but add to the worry of what would happen when I walked through the door of my home.

There was no point in running away from my parents, so the fear was slowly suffocating me as we got close. I didn't have the heart to go on. Frankly, I wanted to sleep under the slide in the park like we did a few years ago. Amrit had broken Mama's favorite vase, and his fear of the imminent consequences had led our little group to take refuge in the park. How he dragged us there, I have no idea, but it was no different than the sleepovers that had been a staple from my childhood.

"God help us," I muttered under my breath as we stopped in front of Ali's house. He pulled away from my brother and attempted to stand by himself, succeeding only with the help of the rail.

Amrit pushed me forward as he spoke. "Not it!"

"That's not fair!" I whispered back. He put his hand on my shoulder, his face solemn.

"You're the youngest."

I was about to refute when I heard a quiet voice beside me. "I'll do it." Naina was pale and terrified, but she had more courage than any of us. "I'll do it." She let out a shaky breath and was about to step forward when I shook my head, annoyed at myself as I came to a realization.

"You're all covered in blood, and you," I turned to Ali, "look terrible." I pointed a finger toward my brother.

"But you owe me, Veere." He smiled despite the fear in his eyes as I turned around. I fisted my trembling hands and stepped forward. *God help me.*

I knocked on the door.

A tense silence hung in the air in the moments after our detailed explanation. The anger radiated from all sides toward the couch the four of us had retreated to. I didn't dare look at either of my parents, but I was sure that I would get my fair share when we finally returned home. Aunt Inaya, Ali's mother, was the first to break the silence.

"Have you eaten?"

I glanced at the others and shook my head to collectively respond for the group.

"No," I said quietly.

She turned away as she began to cry, and Uncle Mihran comforted her.

"It's time to go." My father's voice had grown colder than it had been in years, and we knew better than to talk as we got our things and left. Naina left with her father, who seemed more relieved than angry, and we followed soon after.

The walk home was short, and when we passed through the door, finally out of the cold, the tension between us seemed to have grown. My father turned to my brother, angrier than I had seen him in a long time, and his hand raised almost instantly. It hung there for what seemed like an eternity before it fell limp at his side. Mama and Papa had never done anything more than yell and throw the occasional shoe, so the action spoke to how much we had truly messed up. Papa turned away and followed my mother into the kitchen. I glanced at Amrit.

"What do we do?" I whispered. He narrowed his eyes at me.

"Why do you think I would know?" If we had been at any other point in time, I would have laughed, but instead, I opted to glare.

"You're the troublemaker, and you've lived longer." I hit his arm as I yelled quietly at him. "Use your experience to gauge how much we messed up." I glanced at my trembling hands.

"Out of ten?"

I went stiff as our heads turned towards a sudden noise. It was muffled and muted, but it was the only thing that could have made me feel any guiltier than before, the sound of my father's tears.

"Ten," he whispered.

My mouth went dry as my vision blurred. I had only ever seen my father like this once before, and it was years ago when I still held onto the innocence that came with a happy childhood. My jaw ticked as I looked again at my brother.

"This is all your fault."

I turned away and went to my room before he had a chance to reply. I blamed him for the tension, but I had taken to blaming myself for the rest of it. I had chosen to follow him, even though I knew it would lead to this, but oddly enough, I would do it again if I had to. Ali was alive, Naina

27

was back with her father, and my parents, despite their hours of worry, were still here. Everyone had made it back safely.

I closed the door behind me and let my head fall against the chipped paint as I collected my thoughts.

I'm sorry.

Present Day

CHAPTER FOUR

Courage and Forgiveness

The day passed calmly, and another came before I could get used to the comfort that accompanied a time without worry. We returned to the fields to tend to the land and help it grow. The sun brought with it warmth, for the time being, but it would soon grow to become oppressive with the summer. A season that once marked freedom was now nothing more than a time to overcome and bear together.

"I can finish up," Amrit said. I glanced over at him and shook my head. Sweat had beaded over his skin, and his breathing, though not heavy, wasn't as light as it usually was. It was nearly midday, and he was ready for the moon to make its appearance. We all were.

"I can do it."

"I know, but you're bleeding, dummy. Let me finish." I looked down at the seeds in my hand and continued the work that had given me apparent purpose. It was the only reason I was here, and it refused to release its hold on me.

"Meher," he prompted.

"You missed a spot," I said, ignoring the urgency that laced his tone as I focused instead on the soil. It would

29

nurture the seeds and help them sprout in the coming months. His hand pressed against my back before he stepped to stand in front of me, his hand covered with the blood that was the cause of his worry.

"Please."

I met his gaze and gave a reluctant nod.

"Okay." I gave him the seeds and left to sit on the edge of the field. The guards had recently made their rounds, so there was no reason to worry. Still, there was an ominous feeling in the pit of my stomach.

The sun raised to its highest point, and Amrit had nearly finished when the sound of hooves reached my ears. I stood up as quickly as I could, but the attempt was futile. They had seen me, and now, I had to face the consequences.

I didn't turn to my brother as the guards grabbed me by my arms and pushed me forward. He would blame himself for this, I knew, but I would blame myself for his guilt. I had given into the pain, and now I would pay with my own blood.

"You worthless Terror!"

I was pushed into a cell and chained in a way that made the familiar concrete wall scrape my already rough skin. He would come. He always did. Every mistake, every word misspoken, and he was ready to make it something I would never forget.

I sat back on my knees and let my head fall forward as I prayed. It was the only comfort I could find in a place full of injustice, where the walls bled, and the air was filled with silent screams. I didn't stop until the door to my cell opened, and the sound of familiar footsteps echoed in my ears.

"First, you attack one of my guards, and now, you slack off?" He slammed the baton in his hand against the metal, but I didn't flinch. Instead, I chose to look at the young man who stood by his side, his suit and tie a statement of his wealth, before ultimately looking away. The Overseer raised his baton, and I tensed as I waited for the impact, but it didn't come.

"Son," he spoke lightly, "punish the Bonded." The man's eyes widened at the command.

"Father—"

"Elijah!" The man clenched his jaw and reached for the baton before the Overseer pulled it away, his eyes calculating.

"No. This one deserves worse." He grabbed the whip and put it in his son's hand like a father giving his son his first set of car keys. It looked normal, and I think that was what bothered me the most.

"Go on, son." The man brought up his arm, his hand trembling in the moments before he faltered. I found it in me to raise my head and look him in the eye. This man was not like his father. I suppose it never occurred to me that he could be worse than the Overseer, but I had only ever met one person worse than the man I had been called to serve.

The man's hand fell with unforgiving force, and I flinched at the sudden pain. His green eyes were filled with an emotion that seemed foreign. He hesitated once more before his face hardened, and the change was so quick that I believed I had imagined it.

The pain returned worse than before. The whip sliced through my skin, and again, I was stamped with blood. I took it with the silence I had adopted since the beginning. My heart pounded, and sweat lined my skin, but there was only one thing on my mind. Home. I wanted to go home. I wanted to hug my mother and laugh with my father again. God, I wanted to go home again.

It stopped.

"Father, may I have the room?" The Overseer laughed. It was an eerie sound that echoed in the cell as he patted the man on the shoulder with a proud smile.

"Of course, son."

He waited until the door shut to throw the bloody whip to the floor in what I was sure I had mistaken as disgust. He sat down opposite me and ran a hand through his blond hair. He stayed silent and made no move to speak. Every action was unusual, unexpected. I did not know him, and I didn't want to, but there was something there that had a chance of being meaningful, of being something more than what I had grown used to.

"I'm sorry."

The words, like the emotions, were foreign. His voice was rough; his shoulders slumped forward as if he had been beaten down in my place. He stared at his trembling hands before they clenched into fists.

"I'm so sorry."

I turned, so my shoulder rested on the wall beside me and leaned back despite my new wounds. I didn't trust him; I never would, but there was a part of me that wanted to believe that he was as unwilling as I was to desire a reality like this. He seemed normal, but I suppose, everyone here did.

His eyes glazed over, and for a moment, I thought he was going to cry. He didn't. They never did.

The man didn't speak. There was nothing to say, but still, so much was left unsaid. His story differed from my own, but the two stood parallel, like two sides of a coin. One could not have one side without the other, but I wondered if there was a need for either.

He stood after a few minutes and stepped through the door of the cell, looking back for only a moment as if to speak, before turning away again. I was led back to the cabins shortly after his departure. I looked ahead once I had been left alone to watch the sunset. The dawn covered the sky in a way that made it seem as though the world was burning. It alluded to the thoughts residing in the deepest corners of my mind and affirmed that the fire of this poisoned world had finally spread and the sky had finally fallen.

I stopped at the cabins for a new pair of clothes before I went to the showers. I twisted the knob and stood under the shower head as the water washed away the blood from my clothes and cleaned the gashes. My breathing grew uneven as the seconds passed, but I stood there in the darkness, shivering in the cold as I coped with the pain before it numbed. I washed the dirt off my face and hands and cleaned what I could before the water turned off. I waited the remainder of the hour by the cabin for the others to return.

The men walked together, and many failed to notice me as they entered the place they knew now as their only refuge. Naina walked amongst them, hidden until her eyes fell on me. She went to grab what medicine we could spare and whatever supplies were available before we retreated to the small area behind the cabin. I pulled up my shirt and slumped forward. She cleaned the wounds and bandaged the bottom half of my back, where most of the gashes were, before wrapping the wound on my arm. Her silence was expected, but it was unlike her usual joyous nature. She would always smile before, but now she did her best to hold in the tears that always seemed to pool into her dim eyes.

"I saved your lunch," she mentioned, but Naina didn't stand until after she was satisfied with her work.

"I'll take these to Miss Yuna tomorrow." She finished folding my torn clothes, and I hummed, tired of the day and eager for the only escape we had.

We walked back to the cabin together and sat at our spot in the corner. Ali and Amrit were already there, waiting patiently for us so that we could eat the bread and soup that would be our dinner. I broke my lunch into four parts and shared it with the others before we said our thanks and began.

The little light we had soon dimmed, but the moon shined to offer light when there was none. I laid down beside the others on the blanket I called my bed and looked up at the ceiling, imagining the clouds drifting over the park my family would often go to. We would run around in the grass, trying to catch each other before being called to go back home. The world was so much brighter then. Now, I was left to do nothing but wonder what had happened. I looked over to Amrit before closing my eyes as sleep tugged at the corners of my consciousness.

"It's not your fault," I spoke softly into the air.

None of this was anyone's fault. We were all trying to survive in a world that believed our very existence was an injustice to them. We were different, so by consequence, we were below a society that had put themselves on a pedestal. They trusted their own more than they trusted us because we were still trying to make a place for ourselves, a name, an identity, anything. My people came here with nothing to find a better life, and I was left to deal with the outcome of their decision. I wasn't here because I wanted to be. I was only here because there was nowhere left for me to go.

Seventeen Days Before Independence Day

CHAPTER FIVE

An Apology

An unnatural silence had taken hold of my home, and it remained for the coming days. I rarely left the security of my room, but when I did, my eyes stayed glued to the worn, wooden floor. My guilt weighed most heavily during dinner when I was forced to face my parents. It was at moments like this that I found it hard to breathe. Guilt had taken me by the heart in a way it never had before, and I could barely stop thinking about the pain I had caused them, how I hurt them in a way that led my father to cry. The sound echoed in my ears as I sat at the table, and what appetite I had, disappeared. I stood quietly.

"Excuse me." My soft voice was enough to fill the room.

"Sit down."

I glanced at my mother before taking a seat, and for the remainder of the hour, I pushed around the food on my plate as I tried to choke down what I could. The anger I had maintained toward my brother remained constant, so the past few days had been lonely, but I had befriended the characters in my books and lived their lives in a feeble attempt to escape my current situation.

"Meher."

I looked my mother in the eye for the first time in days before ultimately looking away.

"Eat." My plate was the only one still filled with food.

"I'm not hungry."

I stood up with both my plate and my brother's before heading toward the kitchen. It was Amrit's turn to wash the dishes, so that meant that I was free to return to my room. I faltered at the thought and opted to go to the one place that refrained from holding its silence.

I stepped out into the cold and welcomed the chill that came with the wind. The branches rustled in the shadows, and I was left to stare at the stars sprinkled over the midnight sky. I stood in the flickering light of the streetlamp with my head in the clouds. My thoughts wandered away from my life and toward one of the many futures I had imagined for myself. I closed my eyes and let my head fall back. In this one, I lived in the clouds and took care of the stars before they fell asleep. I knew the Man on the Moon, and we would grow to become good friends. He would soon introduce me to the Winds so I could learn how to fly during the day. I would travel the world and watch the seasons from my place in the sky. I would be a part of the world, more so than what I was now.

My mind was too occupied to notice the person who had joined me in the cold. He offered me a coat.

"Let's take a walk."

I trailed behind my father as we circled the neighborhood. I didn't think he would notice I had fallen behind until we had reached the end of the street, but no more than a second had passed before he stopped to walk beside me.

"How have you been?"

"Good." My feet crunched over the thin layer of fallen snow. "How is work?"

"It's as good as it can be."

A piece of the tension had faded away, but much remained. There was one thing I truly wanted to say, but I couldn't speak much more than I already had. He stopped to check his watch a few minutes later.

"We should head back before your mother starts to worry."

I entered my home with pink highlighting the tips of my ears. I slipped off my shoes as the warmth returned and followed Papa to the kitchen when he called for me.

"Take a seat." I sat down with my hands under my legs to warm them as I waited for what I expected to be a verbal reprimand. My father would scold me, and maybe, I could finally rid myself of the guilt that had plagued me for so long.

My heart pounded unusually quickly in the moments before his return. I had never seen him act like this before, albeit I had never done anything to cause such an action, but I worried. My father stepped out of the kitchen and slipped a plate of rice and beans in front of me as he sat down to my left.

"Neither of us is leaving until you finish eating." I glanced at him before looking away.

"I—"

"We'll talk after you finish." He handed me a spoon. "Eat up," he said softly.

I cleared my throat, stared at the mountain of food before me with resolve, and began eating. Papa waited until I had finished before offering me a glass of water. He leaned back into his chair with his arms crossed, and just like that, the tension had returned.

"When I was your age, I reveled in my freedom. My parents never interfered much with my life. They never asked me where I was going or when I would be home, but they never taught me about the world, so I had to teach myself all the lessons I've taught you. I didn't trust them to help me." He sighed. "That was my mistake, but I always thought you knew that you could come to us with your problems."

"I'm sorry." I let out a shaky breath as I pushed back my tears. I had taught myself to keep it in and hold it, but it never worked with my father. He was too genuine, and it made it difficult to pretend.

"I-I didn't mean to—" I choked out a sob as the guilt overcame me.

My father hugged me, his expression worried despite his earlier relief, and he let go only after I had grown quiet. I wiped my cheeks dry with the back of my sleeves.

"You're at an age where the world is still new. You're going to make mistakes, and it's okay." He smiled faintly. "I just want you to know that your mother and I are here for you when you do."

He handed me a box of tissues as the tears returned.

"Trust us from now on, okay?"

"Okay," I breathed out. My father gave a large, wholesome smile.

"Good. Now, go straight to bed. I better not catch you with your head in a book." He smiled and kissed my forehead before he left. I stole a small chocolate bar from the kitchen before I followed him up the dark stairs. I stopped in front of my brother's door and stood there, pondering the idea of extending a white flag, before I let out a tired sigh and walked in.

Amrit was playing an old video game my parents had gotten him years ago. The sound was off, but he was too occupied to notice me until I hit him over the head with the chocolate bar.

"What was that for?" he whispered. He glanced between the clock by his bed and the game.

"Can't sleep?"

"No." I was too awake even to bother trying, and Papa had taken away my liberty to read. That was what I told myself, but I knew my anger at him was taking its toll on me, and I wanted things to go back to normal.

I sat down on the floor beside my brother and watched him play. He gave up trying to pass the final level after a quarter of an hour, so he tossed his game up on the bed behind us and leaned back against the footboard. I did the same.

"You should have listened to me."

"I know," he said. A short silence followed before he said the two words that would be enough to reconcile our friendship.

"I'm sorry."

I offered him the chocolate bar with a small smile.

"Took you long enough, Veere. I was getting bored all by myself." He laughed as he broke off two pieces.

"I was busy."

"Busy," I deadpanned. "With what?"

Something in his demeanor had changed. I had been too young to notice, then, but I remember the sorrow in his eyes and how his mind seemed to be elsewhere. I should have known that the day meant more to him than what presently gave it value. It was the anniversary of her death, and it was something I should not have forgotten.

He laughed hopelessly.

"Nothing."

I grabbed his arm before he could stand up, and the action was enough to catch his attention before he could look away.

"What is it?"

"It's nothing," he breathed. I didn't push him any further, but he gave in regardless. Amrit reached under his bed and pulled out a small shoebox filled with old memories. He took out a worn piece of paper, a list. He had written it ten years ago when he was eleven. It was right before the incident; in the years everything began to change. I was too young to recall much, but he remembered every second of it.

He remembered how he had been walking with his little sister to go home from school and how he had let her trail behind as he talked with his friends. It was his fault, he believed, that she tripped over a rock and stumbled onto one of the higher members of society. It was his fault that the man hit her so hard that she fell onto the Aryan woman behind her, and it was his fault that the woman's family took offense, and by consequence, dragged his little sister into an alley and beat her until Amrit could barely recognize her. He had been too afraid of them to fight back, and he blamed himself for her death to this day. All I could do was hope he would find a way to forgive himself.

"I tried to write her a letter." His eyes glazed over. "I thought that I could finally do it this time too, but I can't." His voice broke.

"You don't know what to say?"

He shook his head.

"I'm worried that she won't forgive me."

I looked down at my hands. I had seen death, but I had never experienced it for myself. It had kept itself away from me at that time, so there was no way that I could understand his pain.

All I could do was offer comfort the only way I knew how.

I pointed to the open window, and he turned around to look at the star I had taken a sudden interest in, the North Star, Polaris.

"I think she's watching over us and that she's already forgiven you. I think she's in a better place, where it's warm, and the flowers are always in bloom. If it makes a difference,

I think she's happy and that she's waiting for us to join her, wherever she is."

His eyes were stuck on the stars that kept the darkness from taking over the night, and when he spoke, he seemed to have let go a little more.

"Take care, Ajooni."

Present Day

CHAPTER SIX

Comfort and Rain

The soil was damp under my bare feet, and the soft drizzle that was the morning rain accompanied the grey clouds that drifted overhead. We were working in the barn today, and a part of me was disappointed. I loved the rain. I spared an occasional glance outside, wistful as the clouds covered the sky.

"Lunch is ready."

I glanced at Amrit and followed him to where the other men were sitting. I could see the guilt in his eyes, but we would never address it. He would forget with time and move on. He had to. There was no way to change what had happened, so all we could do was prepare for what was to come.

I took the sandwich Yua offered me before I sat down.

"Thank you."

She gave me a small smile that shone brighter than the bruises that covered her skin. I didn't know who had it worse, but I kept my head down and lived quietly. It was the only way I knew how to survive.

We ate quietly. There was nothing to say, and we embraced the silence. We had laughed yesterday, and that was enough to be thankful for, so I took the comfort that came in the presence of family while I could.

A young girl walked through the barn doors without an umbrella. She stopped in front of the Bonded who were eating on the floor with her hands folded in front of her. She studied us for a moment before her voice filled the room.

"May I have some assistance with the horses?"

I glanced at the others and stood up as I put the last bite in my mouth. Everyone else was still eating.

I led her to the stalls and crossed my arms as I waited behind her. Her attention went straight to a black mare, Midnight. She was more benevolent than the other horses and notably calmer. The girl opened the gate and took out Midnight with considerable ease. She knew what she was doing, that much I had figured out from her posture, but the only thing I was yet to understand was why she had called me here to help her when she clearly needed none.

She led the mare outside and readied her for a ride. I stood there watching her for a few moments and nearly left to return to the barn when she started speaking.

"Do you mind joining me?" I looked at her, confused. She was asking. They never asked. We weren't worthy of choice, only direction.

"I have work to do." There was nothing left to say, so I turned to leave.

"Please." I froze at the word. "I have no one to talk to."

Honestly, I didn't know what to do. The decency that lingered in my heart told me to go, promising that not every person who stood on the other side was there of their own choosing, but I knew better. Still, I hesitated.

"Do me this one kindness."

My jaw ticked, but I had already made up my mind.

"Alright."

She smiled, and I followed her onto the pasture at a distance. I trailed behind in a way that resonated with our relationship. Master and slave, silver spoon and no spoon, perfection and defective. We were not the same, and we never would be, so I made sure to act as such. It was always the small things they noticed, like the way we held ourselves when we talked to them or how we looked at them. Every action meant more in a place that had laid its foundation on power and hierarchy.

"I started riding when I was a girl. My brother and I would always spend hours in this field with our horses." She looked back at me and slowed down.

"Have you ever been on a horse?"

I shook my head. "No."

I took in the shifting clouds and savored the sprinkle that was the rain. The leaves rustled in the wind and drops of water weighed down the blades of grass. It was the quiet before the storm.

"Would you like to try riding?"

"No."

She looked around. "You can talk to me freely. There is nothing to fear."

46

The corner of my lip raised in a small smile. "I'm not afraid." Pain was always close by, and the end didn't scare me anymore. Death would consume me eventually, so what if it were today instead of tomorrow. It wouldn't matter in the collection of memories that was my life.

"Are you angry?" she asked, trying to figure out the meaning behind my short words.

"No."

She frowned as she thought.

"Not angry?" She glanced at me, curious as I took the reins from her hands and stepped away. I had noticed people approaching us from a distance.

The Overseer approached us with a woman I saw frequently, though briefly. Her blonde hair was pushed up in a tight bun, and her violet dress hovered over the wet grass. Guards trailed behind the two but did not interfere. It was not their place to be anything more than bystanders.

"Your mother has been looking for you. She bothered me; do you understand that, Willow?" He was composed, but there was fire in his eyes, and though it seemed otherwise, his anger was not aimed at her but the woman standing beside him.

"She is not my mother."

He sighed. "I have work to do, dear. Be nice." He spared me a glance but continued toward the barn to check on the other Bonded. The woman waited until he could no longer hear her before she stepped forward with a glare.

"You will treat me with respect," she demanded.

"Never."

The woman raised her chin as she backhanded the girl I hardly knew.

"You wretch! Such a terrible child. It's a wonder your father cares for you." She wrinkled her nose in disgust before walking away. I helped the girl up and stepped away, ignoring the tears in her eyes because there was nothing I could do.

She dusted herself off before glaring in the woman's direction. Her eyes were filled with an emotion I was too familiar with. Hatred.

The girl wiped away a tear before running away. I watched her go, unsure. I had only seen her from afar, wandering here and there and, at times, laughing with the guards, but I had never talked to her before today. It was a stupid thought; one I was sure would bring more of the pain that had filled so much of my time here. She was the Overseer's daughter. A friendship with her would be senseless and nothing, if not completely foolish, but I had considered these thoughts too late. I had already seen her as human.

The rest of the day passed by normally, and the night came quickly. The guards had stayed away because of the rain, and the Overseer, aside from that single visit, had opted to remain in the comfort of his estate. We had nearly finished eating dinner when I voiced the thought that had been on my mind.

"I met the Overseer's daughter today."

The three of them shared a glance as they ate. "The girl?" Amrit asked.

I nodded.

"How was she?"

"Decent," I said.

"That's a surprise." Ali said as he chugged down his glass of water. Naina took it when he finished, and he thanked her with a small, lopsided smile.

"Be kind to her," I said.

Amrit's lips fell into a frown.

"Meher—"

"She's young, and her mother hits her."

"Her father beats you. He beats us and everyone else here. They don't deserve your compassion. After everything they've done—" he started. His voice grew louder as he watched me with disbelief. I looked down at the wooden floor, unsure if the request was anything short of insane, but I couldn't forget the pain in her eyes because it did not echo the reality I lived today.

"Just be kind to her, please." He watched me for a moment with hard eyes before agreeing.

"Okay."

Naina smiled at me, but there was no joy. Only sadness occupied her eyes as she watched me go. I walked through the cabin door and sat down on the wooden steps, basking in the cool air for a moment before I let my shoulders slump forward, wondering if this would ever change, if I could ever go home again.

I rubbed my tired eyes and tensed when the door opened. Amrit sat down beside me.

"I'm sorry," he said. "I shouldn't have yelled at you."

I looked out onto the fields.

"It's so hard, sometimes," he continued. "All of you are always covered in bruises, and I can't do anything about it."

His voice was low as he clasped his hands together and let out a shaky breath.

"I'm just afraid that one day, you won't come back." He shook his head. "I ... I can't—"

He cried silently into the air, and the thunder was kind enough to cover the action with fervor. I put my arm around his shoulder and pushed back the tears that came to my eyes at the sight of his.

"We'll get through this, Veere," I said with a small smile. "Then we can finally go back home."

It began to pour as the rain decided to make its last appearance for the next few days. The door opened again, and the two of us were pushed forward.

"Group hug!" Naina yelled as I laughed and steadied myself. Ali smiled and turned around so the four of us could do what we often did before we parted ways. It was a way to forget the world that surrounded us and pretend nothing mattered but the present. The action was akin to a final goodbye that hid a promise in its familiarity. *I will see you again.*

We pulled away from each other, and quiet laughter filled my ears as we sat back.

"One more day," Naina said with a soft smile as we looked up into the sky. "Just one more day."

The words had become the precept of our epic. If we could get through today, then we would get through tomorrow. It didn't matter how hard or painful things became. We would wait. We would get through it because one day, life would be worth living.

Fifteen Days Before Independence Day

CHAPTER SEVEN

Until We Meet Again

The coming days passed in a blur, and before I could acknowledge the comfort of having a brother, it was time for him to leave again. He packed his bag and left his room nonchalantly as he headed into the kitchen. He had grown used to the back and forth between home and university, but I didn't have the same luxury. I stayed still, waiting as he lived his life. It was bothersome enough to know that despite the lack of opportunity for our people, he would always have more freedom than I did. He was a man living in a world created by men, so he could hope for a future of his own.

It was disheartening to know that my mother held a job when I knew that I never could. She worked in a field that required experience, and it was the only reason she was able to hold onto her job after the war. I could never have the independence she did, which was something I had come to terms with, but I didn't know what to think when the future remained unknown. I would have to marry well, I suppose, but I wanted to do more than stay home. My father knew as much, so whenever the topic of my future was brought into question, he remained quiet.

Mama was different. She would try to help me understand that it was the reality I had to live with and that it would be harder for me if I fought against it. She wanted me to have a comfortable life, and while I was grateful, I knew that I could never live without the freedom I had experienced in my youth. It wasn't a question of my preference but rather the reality of my very existence. I wanted more from life than happiness in the years of my ignorant youth, and the thought was more foolish than I could believe I had ever been.

"Where were you?"

"Sleeping," I answered as I sat down at the table. "School starts on Monday for me too, you know."

"Ah, high school," he sighed. "Those were the good old days." I laughed, knowing well that high school meant something different for me. I enjoyed learning, but the people were not as welcoming.

Amrit had a very different view of life than I did. He flowed with the world like a river and surpassed its expectations. He was happy with the life he had only just begun to make for himself, and he looked forward to the future and its gifts. And while he lived as the water, I lived as the fish waiting for the opportunity to swim away to a place where I wouldn't be pushed back by the current. I craved the freedom to dream of a future I could determine for myself, where I lived life on my own terms. It was imprudent and rash to think this way and much too unrealistic, but it was the hope that things would change that kept me going.

"When are you leaving?"

"Ten minutes," he said. "I have to catch the train out of the city."

"Do you have to go?"

He put his arm over my neck playfully before returning to his cereal.

"I'll be back after I take my exams. It'll only be a few weeks."

It was only a matter of time, but things changed as time moved on, and nothing remained certain. It was an unreliable thing, but we were foolish enough to believe that we had it under our control. I knew the truth, however, and it was only a matter of time until the world fell apart at the seams.

We finished our breakfast and went outside to say our goodbyes. Ali and Naina met Amrit on the driveway and joked about how he had only just arrived. My parents didn't have the heart to do much more than laugh as he picked up his things.

I walked my brother to the edge of the road and engulfed him in a hug as my father backed the car.

"Study hard." *And live for the both of us*, I wanted to say.

"Take care of them for me." *And make sure they don't feel lonely when we're both away.*

The words meant more than we expressed, but we knew each other well enough to understand what had been left unsaid. He wanted me to take care of our parents, and I wanted him to take care of himself. The world had left us divided again, and we could do nothing but hope the future had kept our dreams in mind.

Five Days Before Independence Day

CHAPTER EIGHT

A Past Forgotten

The wind knocked against the waves below us, and every so often, water would sprinkle over my old shoes. Papa stood next to me in his black coat, and together, we watched the world. Amrit had left again, and Mama was busy catching up with Aunt Inaya, her childhood friend, so like old times, we returned to the Washington Bridge.

"Papa?" I asked. He hummed.

"Why did God make us defective?" He looked up at the sky, his thoughts hidden behind the turmoil in his eyes.

"He didn't. He just made us too different for the world to handle."

His honesty tore away every facade, every barrier he had put between us. Papa was often realistic and his emotions, however painful, were never kept from me. I was more like him than I could ever comprehend, and it was this similarity that had made him into something more like a brother than a father. He had his moments, of course, but we laughed more often than we fought, and ever since Amrit had first left for university, I had grown accustomed to his company.

"You know, when I was in the war, I was a big hotshot."

55

I laughed. "Really?" A part of me couldn't believe it.

"Oh, yeah," he said. "General Griffin was a good friend of mine. He wouldn't do anything without my input."

I shook my head. "I would have believed you if you said it was General Andrews, but Griffin? *The* General Griffin."

"He was different then." Nostalgia lined his otherwise dejected tone.

"Human?"

Papa shrugged. "He lost his son in the war."

The words sparked a different type of frustration in my soul. He defended a man who used to be a friend, and that much I understood, but General Griffin had done more than make a simple mistake. He began a movement that had changed the very shape and color of this country. He had betrayed his people, and by consequence, betrayed humanity itself. He had killed thousands for something as futile and transient as power, so I felt no remorse for the man, and I didn't believe that I would ever learn to forgive him.

"You lost your brother," I argued. He sighed wearily and looked out at the water as he struggled to change the topic of conversation.

"How's school?"

It was my turn to sigh, and Papa laughed. "Did I hit a sore spot? I thought you liked school."

"I'm taking my final exams tomorrow."

"That's rough, kid." He gave me a pat on the back. "But if you put in enough effort now, you'll be better off when you graduate."

I looked away and let my gaze wander.

"No one will hire me either way."

Silence took over the space between us, and despite the continuous sound of the passing cars and roaring waves, it was deafening. The truth had such an effect. We could pretend to live in the world before the war, in America before it was divided. It was nearly impossible for a colored woman to get a job in the city, so I had no future. Still, it was nice to pretend sometimes.

Papa said to me then that the world used to be a beautiful place and that if I looked away from the crowd, I could see that it hadn't changed, that we had. I didn't understand him then, but I could now. I had lived a little more and seen enough of the world to acknowledge the truth of his words. The grass was still green, and the wind had not yet stopped. The animals continued to live like before as if nothing had changed. In many ways, nothing had. Life would go on without disruption, and we would continue to laugh until the Aryans found a way to silence us again.

Present Day

CHAPTER NINE

Hope and Pain

I stood on the tip of my toes and reached for a bowl on the third shelf. My hand barely grabbed it by the edge before I flipped it over and caught it.

"Thank you." I smiled at the woman who had shared her bread with me after my first beating. Her motherly nature was comforting in a place where people looked out only for themselves.

"Anytime, Miss Dae." She urged me to call her by her first name, but it felt unnatural. Growing up in a respectful Panjabi family, I knew that how I addressed someone echoed the amount of respect I had for them, but it meant more to me than it would ever mean to her, so I had compromised.

She continued her work in the kitchen as I went out the door and toward the truck filled with animal feed and bags of flour. Erasto, the unofficial leader of the Bonded here, had given the task to the four of us. He knew that we had a history, so he had done us a kindness by letting us work together.

I picked up a few bags of flour, then a few more until my hands were covered and my lower back had started to ache.

58

Every movement pulled at the scabs protecting my wounds, and I did my best to let them heal, but there was little I could do when there was work to be done.

A few guards laughed as they passed by.

"If only!" they yelled. I looked down at the white flour that covered my hands and arms before turning away.

"Hey, you okay?" Ali pushed back his hair as he picked up a bag, and I echoed his movement with a short laugh.

"Never better."

I helped them finish with the feed and sat down when I was done, my breathing heavy. Ali and Amrit left to check in with Erasto, and Naina took the time to sit down beside me and lean into my shoulder.

"Bhenji?" I asked.

She hummed at the nickname that labeled her as my older sister.

"How much longer?"

Her smile faltered. "I don't know." She took my rough hand between her own and held it quietly.

She drifted off as I stayed confined inside the walls of my mind, and though only minutes had passed, it felt much longer. The silence created a barrier, and the safety that I always felt around my family suddenly felt more real. I could relax, but like all good things, it came to an end too quickly.

A horse in the stables neighed and kicked at the gate of her stall. Naina jumped at the sound and nearly woke up, but I moved her to lean against a barrel as I pulled away. My hand brushed away the strands of stray hair that hung over her face before I rushed toward the noise.

It was Midnight, which did nothing but bother me more. I grabbed her reins and talked to her in an attempt to coax her usual repose, but it was useless. She shook her head a few times and I was about to open the gate to her stable when my eyes fell to her stomach. She started pacing as I stepped away.

"Oh, God." I could barely get the words out. I covered my mouth.

"Oh, my God!" I ran to Naina and shook her awake in my daze. She looked at me with wide eyes.

"Midnight is giving birth." She struggled to stand and fell forward.

"How in the world do you know that?" She pushed herself up and followed me to the stables.

"Look at her stomach." I closed my eyes and took a breath before continuing. "I read a book about horses a few years ago. She's showing all the signs." I rubbed my eyes. "I can't believe I thought she was just gaining weight." For me, the initial shock had worn off, and I had regained my composure. For Naina, it was only just the beginning.

"Oh, my God!" she yelled as she started pacing. "What do we do? How are we supposed to deliver a baby horse? I'm not an animal doctor!"

I frowned.

"A veterinarian?"

She glared at me, and I put my hands up in surrender. Her attention turned to an even more nervous Midnight, and she approached her before eventually turning away.

"We could try to help, but horses are nothing like people. They have four legs, Meher, FOUR!" Her breathing became heavy, and it was at that moment that Ali walked in. I tried to warn him, but everything was met with confusion. Amrit understood almost immediately, so he stayed back to enjoy the show.

"What's going on?" Ali asked.

I sighed and took a few steps back. Naina turned around, and Ali nearly fell back at the abruptness of the action.

"MIDNIGHT IS GIVING BIRTH!"

His face fell, and a forgotten bag of feed fell from his hands at the news. He looked between the two of us, and his mouth fell open in disbelief before he ran an anxious hand through his hair.

"What do we do?"

I waved Amrit over and opened Midnight's gate. He helped her out as I grabbed her reins.

"I don't know!" Naina responded. I led her out into the open and gave her a second to adjust. Naina glanced back at me before turning around completely, her eyes frantic and unnerved.

"What are you doing?"

"Giving her more space. I'm going to take her to the empty supply room in the back." This brought stares from them both.

"You are taking this surprisingly well," Naina said. I glanced between the two of them.

"Somebody has to." Naina took a couple of deep breaths and calmed down before she opened her eyes.

"Okay, so what's the plan?" she asked.

"We let her do her thing and not interfere, I think."

"You think?"

I shrugged.

"From what I can remember, yes."

"Well, you are the most qualified. I'll go tell Erasto." Ali ran off, and Naina left to grab a blanket to make Midnight comfortable. I didn't know if she would be alright with me there, so I got up to leave after she got a little used to the room. She neighed, and I turned around when she started to follow me. I put a hand on her muzzle.

"I'll stay."

"I didn't know that you had befriended a horse." Amrit smirked as he kneeled beside me.

"There's a lot you don't know about me."

He laughed. "Right."

He left, and with him, the majority of my composure. Midnight eased up when I stood by the wall and started pacing again. Naina returned with the blanket and stepped back triumphantly when she had spread it out over the dirt. Ali returned a few minutes later with vague instructions.

"He wants us to stay here."

"That's it?" I asked.

He nodded.

"What do we do?" Amrit asked.

Ali crossed his arms, completely serious. "I have absolutely no idea."

I sat with Midnight because Naina was still in shock, and Ali was terrified. Amrit was clueless, so I did my best to comfort her. My hands were trembling, and I could feel my heart racing, but I was the closest thing to calm she had. She didn't need me, that much I knew, but I aimed to offer her some support.

Despite this, I left after a few minutes and joined Amrit by the stables. The quiet remained for some time before Naina made the bold decision to look past the door. Ali, led by his own curiosity, looked as well.

"Oh, that is disgusting." He heaved and Naina hit his arm.

"It's not that bad." He looked at her with wide eyes, and she gave in.

"Okay, it's bad, but be polite. She can hear you," she whispered. I smiled at the two of them before turning my attention to the world outside.

"We should get some work done, just in case someone comes in."

We spent the next half hour doing odd jobs in the barn and taking turns checking on Midnight and her foal. No one came, however. It was nearly sunset, but still, no one entered the barn. No veterinarian was called, and no one else came to see the newborn. It made me wonder what would have happened if the foal had been a stallion instead of a mare.

"Guys." Amrit ushered us forward. I looked over and followed his gaze as the foal pushed herself up on her legs and stood for what I assumed was the first time. It brought a smile to my face. Ali started crying, and Naina comforted him, but I couldn't move. Amrit leaned against the door with a smile of his own.

"It's just so amazing," Ali sobbed.

I just watched the foal with a heavy heart, knowing that the Overseer would sell her as quickly as he could. He owned the mother, so by default, he owned the foal. She had no right over her child. Not anymore.

It was the way of the world. A mother could not stay with her child because she had a predetermined value. She would be sold and no longer a nuisance. My home state had been one of the last to implement the policies of the Charter, so I had not been here nearly as long as the others, but I had seen it time and time again with the Bonded who had come here with young children. It was nothing short of normal, now. Fathers were separated from their families and children ripped from their mothers' arms. The young were sold and left alone to fend for themselves because the only people who promised to be there couldn't anymore, but it was of no willful choice of their own. There was no decency, no humanity, and nothing left to consider but profit and value and personal gain, but there was nothing we could do. It was the way of this world.

It was rare that I could experience the innocence that came with birth. Death had surrounded me for so long that I had forgotten how pure life was, especially one so new and untainted.

"What should we name her?" Naina asked, excited.

"Hope."

It was out of my mouth before I could realize it, but I didn't take it back. The name suited both the foal and my current situation for one simple reason. Hope was all we had left.

Four Days Before Independence Day

CHAPTER TEN

My Life, Before

The school halls were bustling with students, culture, and color. The lights above flickered in what could be another power outage as the wind knocked against the windows. The muffled thunder of a casual winter storm seeped through the walls and into my ears as I reached my locker. First period would start in ten minutes. Until then, I would only hope that I could get to class without any trouble. Now that, of course, was easier said than done.

The average school day held within it about three major arguments that were enough to grow into proper quarrels. The fights were usually rough, but there was a set of rules that everyone at this school followed. They would be freehand and without weapons, and when one side had either given up or passed out, they would go their separate ways as if nothing had happened. Despite the differences in belief, and often, the distinction of color, there was a type of loyalty connecting the students of this place. We all belonged to the other side of humanity, and while many believed in the inequality that held with variation, we let this glue us together.

The people here were not the same and not equal by any means, but we were different from the Aryans, and nothing would change their noble superiority.

I had never been inherently careful, but it was in my very nature to be subconsciously perceptive. That was the only reason I noticed three people huddled around someone near the bathrooms. In the midst of the crowd, it was easy to miss, but I happened to see what was otherwise hidden. A student who looked Aryan was receiving hatred for something he had not done. It was a boy I recognized as a friend.

Noah's golden hair glinted in the light. He was the only person with blond hair and light skin in this entire school, the only one who looked enough like them to bring himself any attention.

My feet moved towards him before my mind could process the action. I was never one to interfere unless someone from my group, my family, was involved, but he was a friend and the only person I knew who had still managed to hold onto his innocence. He never fought with anyone and rarely spoke as it was, but if I was going to do this, which I suppose had already been decided, I needed to acknowledge the smoldering fact that would determine my mindset for the remainder of the morning. No one would come to save me. Naina had to finish a project before school, which meant that she was already in class, and Ali never had any morning classes, so he was probably helping his parents open their grocery store.

I stepped in front of Noah's shaking form. Whether or not he was at fault, I knew that he didn't deserve this.

"Leave him alone."

The four of them laughed in response. They were too surprised to believe that I could actually be serious, and it was this underestimation that would lead to their downfall. Noah moved his arms away from his head and looked up at me. His sea-blue eyes were tearful and more afraid than I had been in a long time.

"Let him go," I repeated, my voice calmer than before.

"What if we don't?" Tristan, a well-known fourth year, glanced at his friends before turning back to me. "What are you going to do, little girl?"

He grabbed my shirt and pulled me forward, but I punched his cheekbone before he could do any harm. He stumbled back, and one of his people caught him. The other two stared at me in surprise before running forward. I slipped between them and pushed them both into the wall behind me before they could turn around. Tristan's fist collided with my jaw, and the impact sent me to the floor. I groaned but quickly jumped to my feet before his foot could hit my abdomen. I put my fists up, ready, and dodged Tristan as he lunged at me. He hit the wall and put a hand over his face as he turned around with a crooked nose. His eyes were raging and his breathing heavy as he met my gaze.

The bell rang.

My hands fell as we parted ways rather peacefully. If the fight was to continue, it would be after school because, no matter our differences, we always followed the seemingly ancient laws of war that we had adopted at this school. Class periods mirrored nighttime, so all conflict would cease until sunrise.

I picked up my backpack from the floor and waited as Noah stumbled to his feet.

"A-Are you okay?" he asked softly. I glanced at his bruises and nodded.

"It's just a scratch."

"Thank you."

"Anytime."

We went our separate ways. I had English, and he had a science class a few rooms down, so I turned around and listened to the echo of footsteps in the silence. I stopped before the door and waited until my breathing had slowed down before walking in.

It was another world inside, one with the protection that the walls of a classroom often offered for me. I could forget the inequality of society and learn the inner workings of nature and the written word. Education did as much for me as money did to those above me. It gave me power, and though that was not something I desired, it was something I needed to live in my reality. My identity gave me power in my family, my strength gave me equality in this community, and my knowledge allowed me to stand face to face with those above me. It was because I had come to realize that I was as human as them, though I would grow to question that thought, but it was enough for me to disregard the current workings of modern society.

It made me believe that I was not less than them because people were more than their color or power. Character was invaluable, kindness immeasurable, and faith invincible when estimating the worth of a person. Value was less superficial than the physical or financial attributes of someone acknowledged in the life I currently lived.

My belief was not shared with those around me, but I still appreciated the thought that I could dream of a future akin to my beliefs.

I learned quickly that it was not enough to dream and that money was more valuable than character. The world had been recreated in the image of the powerful, and I was nothing more than a stain on their beautiful white nation.

Present Day

CHAPTER ELEVEN

Balance and Deliberation

It had been so long since I last heard music. Whether it be the tune of a song or its forgotten lyrics, they seemed lost in the chaos of the world. Naina would hum the lullaby her mother sang to her as a child when she couldn't sleep sometimes. The sound was enough to wake me, but it was always something I appreciated. To wake up and, for a moment, feel as if I was home again.

So much had changed, it seemed, but the outside world had stayed the same. It was reliable because the wind still blew in all four directions and the flowers still bloomed. The trees remained rooted to the ground, and the birds still lived in their branches. The colored leaves had fallen, but they would grow again.

"What are you most thankful for?"

I set my shovel aside and caught my breath as I stared at Naina.

"What?"

She looked around to make sure no one was nearby before repeating her question.

"What are you most thankful for? Come on; it'll help with your mood."

I laughed lightly as I pressed the shovel into the grass.

"What's wrong with my mood?"

"You've been gloomy ever since yesterday."

My smile fell as I thought back. The Overseer had found a seller and, despite knowing that the foal was still too young to be separated from her mother, she would be leaving next week. Naina stopped working and turned towards me completely.

"What are you thankful for?"

I crouched down and planted a flower. The Overseer's wife wanted to redecorate the entire front lawn in a matter of days, and we were lucky enough to be tasked with the duty. Note the sarcasm.

"The wind," I said. "It's hot, so I'm grateful that the wind is kind enough to cool us off. And the clouds." I pointed to the sky. "They cover the sun every so often and offer the shade I can't get here out in the open."

She listened quietly as we worked. "Go on."

I continued at her words, feeling less disheartened than before. I thought quietly. "I'm thankful that the soil is soft and that I have someone to talk to."

"And?"

I looked around. "And?"

"Are you thankful for anything else?" She nudged me, and I shrugged.

"That's all I can think of." She hit my shoulder with her glove, and I laughed.

71

"I'm thankful for you and Ali and Amrit." I rubbed the back of my neck. "I guess I should have started with that one."

"Yeah, you should have." She glanced at me with a smile as she pressed down the soil.

"Feeling better?"

"Yeah."

A woman's cold voice reached my ears, and the sliver of normalcy I had found disappeared as I slipped back into my regular facade. Naina followed me similarly, knowing too well that any connection to another person would be used against us. It was an insult to the Overseer, I had heard. We were bound to the Charter and, in turn, the Overseer, who stood over us with his foot on our throats. We weren't allowed to make relationships because we belonged to him, not ourselves. No one took the unsaid rule to heart, but we played the role and kept up the act for each other's sake.

"The supervision of their work is imperative. They're too stupid to understand instruction once, so it would do you well to be attentive." I recognized both her voice and the one that came after.

"Yes, Regina."

The woman's posture went rigid. "I am your mother."

"No, you're not. You will never take her place," Willow replied carelessly.

"Well, it's not hard to replace the dead." I could practically hear the smirk in Regina's voice as she spoke.

"Oh, that woman," Willow muttered furiously, though she did nothing to follow her as she did before. She instead chose to do as she was told and supervise us.

"Hello!" Willow said cheerfully. I glanced up and returned the greeting with a nod. "Would you like some help?" she asked as I stood.

I refused with wide eyes.

"No."

Her smile faltered for a second before it returned. The wind picked up again, and strands of her blonde hair fell over her eyes as it passed. She sat down and held a blade of grass between her fingers.

"It looks amazing so far."

"Thank you." She nodded, thinking of something else to say.

"Isn't summer wonderful? It's always been my favorite," she said as I took off my gloves to air out my chafing hands.

"Yes, it certainly is."

"What's your favorite season?"

"Autumn." She stood up to look at the flowers.

"Why is that? It gets so cold."

"I like the cold." It was better than the heat that made my shirt stick to my skin. She reached over and plucked a stray daisy before walking back to me.

"I picked this for you as a token of our friendship!" I took off my other glove as I gazed at the flower. It had only just bloomed. I took it into my bare hands and let it rest over the grass, my eyes closing for a moment as I let myself breathe.

"You don't like it?" she asked.

I stood up and started digging again. "It will wither and die without its roots," I said quietly. I glanced at her as the clouds covered the sun and offered me some relief. She looked dejected.

"Oh, I'm sorry. I didn't know."

Her gaze wandered while we worked, but it didn't take long for her to snap her fingers and run into the Overseer's home.

"I'll be right back!" Naina sighed as she disappeared behind the walls.

"She's nothing but trouble."

"I know."

"And ignorant to the rules of our lives."

"I know."

"She reminds me of you when you were younger."

I shook my head with a small smile. "I was nothing like that as a kid."

Naina shrugged. "I remember it differently."

I looked toward the doors of the house. Its pillars towered over us like skyscrapers, and the white marble covering every inch of the mansion was blinding.

"She's young and naive, but she has a bigger heart than anyone here."

"Maybe that's because it's empty. There's no one else in the estate aside from her family and the guards. She must be lonely." She wiped the dirt off her hands and rested her elbows on her shovel.

"I don't think she knows what we are," Naina said.

"She does, but I don't think she cares."

Willow returned promptly with something hidden between her small hands. She caught her breath before she opened them with a beaming smile.

"I want you to accept this as a token of my friendship." I stared down at the gold chain in her hands. "It was my mother's, but I don't have anything else to give."

I reached forward and closed her fingers over her palm before offering a hand. She took it with a smile.

"Friends?" she asked.

I nodded. "Sure."

"Yes!" She hugged me before running off again. My back ached at the sudden contact, and it had started bleeding again. I watched her as she left, conflicted. She was more innocent than I ever had the chance to be. The world hadn't broken her. It would. It always did, but she had the one thing that had always escaped me. Time.

Eighteen Hours Before Independence Day

CHAPTER TWELVE

Loss and Friendship

"Ali!" Naina yelled at the top of her lungs. I did nothing but stare as she ripped the comforter off him and tossed him a shirt from the closet.

He groaned, the poor soul, and did nothing but feel around for his glasses. I left my spot by the doorframe and handed them to him. He lifted his head and squinted at the two of us before sitting up in his wrinkled and worn batman pajamas. Naina took out a pair of jeans and threw them at him, but I caught them before they could hit his face. I set them down on the foot of his bed as he yawned. She snorted at the pun on one of his graphic T-shirts before turning around with a hoodie in her hands.

"It's six o'clock on a Saturday morning, you guys," he groaned. His rough voice was enough to make her laugh.

"We'll be waiting downstairs," I assured him. He ran a hand down his face as she grabbed my arm and dragged me into the kitchen.

His parents were already awake. Uncle Mihran was reading the newspaper at the table, and Aunt Inaya was making breakfast. They spared us a glance as we rushed down.

"Is he awake, or do I need to drag him out of bed myself?"

I laughed. "That rolling pin is enough to wake a dead man, Aunt Inaya, but don't worry. He's up." She smiled and took the moment to put a plate in my hands.

"Eat before you leave."

"But—" Naina tried to protest.

"Eat!"

We sat down and filled our plates.

"Bhenji?" I said. Naina hummed.

"I have to return a few library books."

"We can fit that in." I never really considered that having knowledge of the schedule beforehand should be a requirement. Knowing her, I should have asked.

We had already finished eating by the time the man of the hour came downstairs. His dark hood covered his messy hair, but the shadow over his face disappeared when Aunt Inaya slammed a plate in front of him. He jumped.

"Ammi!" She hit the side of his head and laughed as she put food onto his plate. Uncle Mihran watched the exchange with a small smile. He was a man of few words, but often, he didn't need to say anything at all.

"Be back before dinner."

I saluted him, the action a joke from when he had to take care of us as kids. Playing military was the only way he could get us to behave.

"Don't worry, Uncle Mihran." Naina leaned forward and whispered for effect, "We'll try to bring him back unscathed." Ali choked on his food and reached for his glass of water. Uncle Mihran chuckled and stood from his seat at the table.

"I'll wake up the twins."

Ali glanced at the two of us and narrowed his eyes.

"What exactly are we doing?"

"What does it matter?" Naina leaned back in her chair. "We already got the okay from your parents." He looked at his mother.

"Why is that not comforting?" he said with a small groan. Naina stood up suddenly, her eyes glued to her watch, and I followed her for the sake of consistency.

"Well, we're leaving. I would hurry up if I were you," she warned as she made her way to the door.

"Be careful."

I nodded at Aunt Inaya's earnest expression and ignored her worry as I always had. We had grown up in this world, so we had made it a habit to be careful. The only thing that separated us from our parents was that we were still trying to enjoy every second of the remnants of our youth. They had already lived through theirs.

I stayed to say goodbye, and the smile I got from his mother was enough to let me go as Ali scrambled to finish the rest of his food. He jumped out of his chair and joined us outside right before the door closed.

The cold wind nicked at my skin, but I didn't mind. It was a sign that winter had come, and that was enough for me. It meant that we could drink hot chocolate next to the fire and play board games when it was snowing. Amrit would come back for winter break, so my books would be left alone for most of the season. It was the only time of the year when the world slowed down enough for us to remember the stories of our lives.

I watched my breath fog up in the air with a smile.

"Let's go! We'll miss it if we don't hurry," Naina said.

We jogged down the sidewalk, and the streetlights shone down on the three of us as we laughed together.

Naina whipped out her trusty bandana.

"Close your eyes."

"I don't think that's—"

I pushed both of his hands behind him, and Naina took the second to tie the cloth around his eyes. I pushed him forward and followed behind as she led him toward the park. Naina kept giggling, which I was sure made him more nervous than anything, but I missed it now, being able to laugh freely and carelessly with nothing at stake but the emotions that filled a single moment.

We reached the park in record time and sat down in our respective swings.

"You can take off your blindfold." He reached for it and blinked a few times before looking ahead.

"Wow."

The sunrise was like a painting. It reminded me of when we had gone camping a few years ago. I nearly set the tent on fire, and Ali almost broke his leg. Naina wouldn't stop complaining about the poison ivy, and Ali's twin siblings,

Leila and Latif, were afraid of the bears and wolves, so my brother had to keep them from crying. Our parents spent the entire weekend trying to figure out how to cook the food they had brought and, in the end, had opted for ordering pizza instead.

"Now what?" he spoke into the morning.

That was the question that I had yet to answer to this day. I had lived, and that was enough. I had laughed carelessly before, and it had lifted the heaviness that threatened to weigh down my heart. I had risen with the sun and fallen with the moon, but it was still dark, and a new chapter had yet to begin. I guess I would just have to wait for the sun to rise again.

Fourteen Hours Before Independence Day

CHAPTER THIRTEEN

Faith

I peeked over the stack of books in my hand and ran forward when I realized that I had fallen behind.

"Where to now?" Naina asked.

"It's just around the corner."

We turned and continued on the sidewalk for a few more minutes before the glorious building came into view. The library. Naina opened the door for us with a small laugh as she watched me struggle. My tower threatened to fall, but I was able to get everything to the front desk before it tipped over.

"You certainly are up early this morning." Ms. Garcia greeted me with a smile, and I returned it before glancing back to make sure Ali was out of ear's reach. I leaned forward and spoke quietly.

"Ali's getting his college decision letter today." She picked up the books and started scanning their barcodes.

"Ah. Which college?"

"The community college a few blocks down."

"Not the main university with your brother?" she asked.

"They aren't accepting any colored freshman this year."

"I heard the community college's colored admission seats have decreased since last fall." I nodded.

"They're only accepting fifty applicants."

She sighed and shook her head before her smile returned.

"You know, when my great-grandmother was growing up, there was no limit on education for people of color and religion." She glanced at him. "But he looks like a smart boy. I'm sure he'll get in."

"I hope he does. He wants to go into medicine."

She set the books aside. "He won't be able to get a job."

My gaze fell. "I know. He's just hoping to get into medical school and start his own practice. That'll be enough."

She picked up *To Kill a Mockingbird*.

"What did you think of this?"

I shrugged.

"It wasn't realistic. I don't think a white man would ever represent a black one. It's a nice thought, though."

She smiled as she put the novel back in the locked cupboard under her desk that she had specifically for banned books.

"What makes you say that?" She was baiting me, I knew, but I responded the same. "Look around, Ms. Garcia," I said softly. "They won't let us shop in the same stores, walk the same streets, all because the color of our skin is darker than theirs."

"And what do you think about that?" She leaned forward on her elbows and waited for me to answer.

"It doesn't make sense to me, but so many people believe it that I think I'm starting to believe it too." I paused, and the question I had longed to ask finally voiced itself. "What did we do to deserve this?"

Her eyes grew distant for a moment. "Nothing." The joy returned to them. "In fact, there was a time when color was celebrated."

I shook my head with a small scoff, doubtful of the concept. "I don't believe it."

She took out a few books and checked them out for me.

"You don't have to believe it happened, just believe that it will, someday." She stacked them up and slid them over.

"Here are a few of my favorites."

"They're all your favorite."

She laughed. "You got me there, dear."

I picked them up and smiled at her. "Tell Mr. Garcia and Miguel I say hello."

"Meher." She stopped me before I could leave. "Do me a favor." My curiosity piqued as I listened. "Keep your heart open. All of them, black, brown, white—it doesn't matter. Keep your heart open."

"Ms. Garcia—" She put a hand on my arm.

"I know that things are getting worse and that it's hard to believe that it will get better, but just remember, we're all human. Time will bring change." I shook my head, but she spoke before I could.

"I've met a lot of people in my life. I've seen more of the world than you know, and I can say with certainty that not all of them are as bad as you think. You're just stuck in between four walls, and I don't want you to fall when they start to crumble." She wore an expression that I, at the time, had no capability to comprehend. "The world is not as dark as you think. When you see the light, don't let it blind you before you can see the brilliance of color."

I walked away, and she watched us go with a gentle gaze. Ali and Naina helped me with my books as we walked home. It was too cold to talk until we passed by his parents' store.

The word *Terror* was sprayed over the door and what was left of the shattered glass windows.

Nothing but the money had been stolen, I had heard, and that was certainly good news.

"That's the second time this month."

"Yeah," he sighed. "I don't know if my parents can afford to fix up the store again.

They're thinking of moving online. It's safer." I hummed, unsure. Most people who shopped here didn't have the resources to shop online, so closing the store would only slow down business.

"My father lost his job!" Naina burst out. Relief overtook her as she let out a breath, but I couldn't help stopping and turning to her with wide eyes.

"What?"

She looked between us. "He got fired Wednesday, and I've tried to tell you both at least a dozen times, but it was so hard. Finally," she sighed. "It's great to get that off my chest."

"Why?" I asked. "He was doing so well." I knew about the late nights and early mornings, and Naina had confided in me more than a few times about her worry, but there was never anything we could say. He was making good money.

"He didn't fit the company's image. That was all they said."

"I'm sorry," Ali said, but she did nothing but smile.

"Don't worry about it," she replied carelessly. "He'll find another job."

I didn't comment on her anxious eyes or restless demeanor. I just walked with her in my usual silence, praying that her family would be okay. The rest of the journey was filled with small conversation and familiar debates until I opened the door.

"I'm home," I yelled. I set my books down on the living room table and went to my parents' office. They were drinking tea and reading what I assumed were research papers and articles. It was their version of a fun time, but I couldn't blame them. I had taken after them as well.

"Waheguru ji ka Khalsa, Waheguru ji ki Fateh." They repeated the greeting and pulled me in for a hug. I sat down on the desk by my father and broke off a piece of his biscuit. He leaned back before he gave me a short pat on the back. I threw him a questioning glance when he pointed to our dastaars. They were the same color.

I high-fived him with a laugh as my mother watched us with a smile. She was sipping her tea when she set the papers aside.

"How was the sunset."

"It was great." Naina walked in and greeted my parents. My mother turned toward the door.

"Did Ali come too?"

Naina nodded. "His zipper got stuck."

My father chuckled. "Of course it did. Did he get the letter yet?"

I shushed him. "He doesn't know it's coming!" I whispered.

Ali walked in and read the room as he glanced around at everyone. "What did I miss?"

"Nothing," Naina said a little too quickly.

"We should go." I muttered a quick goodbye and left to put my shoes on.

"Meher?"

"Yeah, Papa?"

"Your mother and I want to talk to you when you get back home." I stopped what I was doing and stood up as I racked my brain for every mistake I had ever made.

"Am I in trouble?"

"No," he said softly. He put his hand on the side of my head before letting it fall to my shoulder. It was unusual to see him so serious. "There's just something we want to talk to you about."

"Okay."

I left with that, and a sudden nervousness settled deep in my bones.

"You are in so much trouble!" Naina said as we started walking.

"I didn't do anything."

"Are you sure," she asked.

I let out a deep breath.

"No."

"Leave her alone, Naina." He turned to me. "I'm sure it's nothing."

I took his word for it. There was nothing I could have done and nothing I could do now to change anything. I was left to watch my mistakes replay over and over again in my mind. At night, when I couldn't sleep, and my mind drifted, that was all I could do.

I sat up in the darkness with more care than I would ever use during the day. The others would worry if they knew of my pain, and it became harder to deal with when acknowledged, so I ignored it. But it was nights like this one, when every movement brought with it a sharp pain, that I recognized the truth of my reality. Home was a world away, and my family, wherever they were, was even farther out of reach, so all I was left with was an unsatiated longing. I rested my chin on my knee and closed my eyes. The entire world seemed still. It was as if everything had fallen asleep when even the crickets had grown quiet. I could hear my heart beating in my ears and see the moonlight peeking through the gaps in the walls. And, as I sat there in the silent darkness, I could do nothing but hold onto the words of a friend.

Present Day

CHAPTER FOURTEEN

Empathy and Fear

The Overseer had called the Bonded. We were lined up in front of his estate an hour before sunrise with our eyes glued to the ground. Everyone but me, of course. I let my gaze wander as I stood there, the gentleness of an early morning peaceful and comforting, but the world would wake soon with the rising of the sun, and I would soon have to face my reality once more.

Two guards opened the doors for the Overseer, who was standing stiffer than usual. This was enough to pique my curiosity, but nervousness didn't set in until I saw the state of the man. His hair was perfectly combed, and his permanent frown seemed deeper. He stood with strange composure as his eyes studied each and every one of us. I remained calm until I noticed the gun strapped to his side. The Overseer was a man of many things, but he was not civil. He savored agony and reveled in the glory that came with innocent blood. He killed, he murdered, but he did not believe in a painless and instant death.

"You will not question me." We never did.

"You will not challenge me." That was a death wish.

"One mistake, one error, and you will never have the opportunity to beg for your lives." I held in a cough.

"Disrespect will not be tolerated." He turned to Erasto with a cold gaze. It was a warning.

"Keep them in line."

"Yes, Master." He spared us a glance before waving us away with a simple gesture.

"Dismissed."

The Bonded turned at his command and left. I followed them back to the cabins to eat breakfast. We never ate breakfast, so as I sat down in my place by my friends, I took a small piece of bread in my hands with gratitude.

"I talked to Dalmar," Amrit said.

"And?"

"The general is coming."

I forgot to breathe. "When?"

"Today." Naina grabbed my arm, her fear apparent as she spoke next.

"Why did he tell you?" Amrit looked away.

"Erasto gave us home duty."

The sun rose, and with it, my restlessness. I didn't fear General Griffin, though he was a man to be wary of. I had been through too much to be afraid of a man who stood on the bodies of so many people, so I chose instead to focus on my growing dislike for him.

"Meher?"

"I'm coming."

I jogged forward to walk beside Naina with a bucket of fresh milk in my hands and slowed down as I followed her through the back door. The kitchen was bustling, with people rushing in all directions to finish their respective tasks. I set down the milk and helped where needed. There was no lunch break and no time to breathe in the hours before the general's arrival. I did my part and continued working even after he had made his appearance. Nothing changed until Miss Dae stepped in front of me with a vegetable sandwich covered in a napkin.

"Take a quick break. I'll call for you when you're needed." I took it with a relieved sigh and stepped outside, thankful for the space and the open air. I sat down on the back steps and rolled my shoulders, eating quietly as my ears took in the rustling leaves and flying birds.

"Hello!" I recognized her by her voice but looked up regardless.

"Hello." Her blonde hair, usually free, was pulled up so it didn't hover over her pale pink dress.

"May I sit with you?"

I shook my head. "It's best if you don't." Her joy faltered.

"All of Father's guards are at the front or inside. They won't see you here if that's what you're worried about." Her hands were clasped behind her back as she shifted back and forth. She reminded me of Leila, and the thought was enough to bring the leniency I never considered anymore.

"Alright."

She sat down a foot away and gazed out at the flowers and trees. The wind returned to move what was an otherwise still picture. It was a reminder that everything here was alive.

Her stomach growled, and she laughed nervously.

"Father, Grandfather, and the other boys are still eating, and I forgot to eat breakfast."

I offered her the second half of my sandwich as I remembered my mother's words.

Sharing is most meaningful when there is little to give.

"Thank you."

I nodded as I continued to sit with her. It was nice to take in the growing chill in the air. Night would come soon, and I would wait for it wholeheartedly.

My gaze fell to the sudden movement on her dress.

"Don't move."

She looked down and nearly screamed. "Get it off! Kill it!"

"You would never kill a butterfly," I said softly. I took the grasshopper between my hands and walked down the steps. I crouched down to let him go before I stood again and returned to my previous seat.

"What did you mean by that?"

I leaned back on my hands and let myself relax as a headache pinched the corners of my mind.

"A grasshopper has every right to live as a butterfly."

People were so blinded by beauty that they forgot to see things for what they were. They defined themselves by color, money and status. They didn't value intelligence unless it led to power or value kindness unless it brightened a public image. They failed to see people for who they were and focused only on what they had achieved or what they could give. People forgot to be grateful, so they choked on their pride until they couldn't breathe anymore. As was the way of the world.

"I've never thought about it like that."

It was just a new perspective, but it had the power to change everything.

I stood up, and my clothes wrinkled in the wind as I ignored the soreness in my bones.

"I should go."

She nodded. "Thank you for the company."

Miss Dae put me to work as soon as she saw me, muttering quietly that she had forgotten I had left. Her sad eyes told me otherwise.

"They've already eaten. All that's left to do is clean up."

Most of the other women had left to take refuge in their cabin before the stars came out, when the world was harsher to them and deceptive with its lingering darkness. I dried the plates and put them away one by one, my mind wandering with the absence of my friends. They had left to help in the barn during my time outside, and a part of me wanted to join them, missing their company, but I enjoyed the momentary solitude.

Miss Dae gave me a stack of plates.

"These go in the dining cabinet outside. Be careful."

I exited the kitchen and went into the dining room. My eyes took in the house out of pure interest. It was mansion-like and decorated with valuable vases and portraits, but there was nothing meaningful. Family photos didn't hang off the walls to remember the past, and scratches didn't mark the floor to stand witness to the days spent running around in the heat of an old game. There was no echo of laughter in the air.

It was glorious and magnificent, but even with its glass chandeliers and gold-rimmed tables, my own home was more valuable than this one could ever be.

I opened the cupboard and put the plates in their places, too far away to listen to the distant conversation in the nearby room.

"Leonardo here has finally become a lieutenant, right under me," the general said.

"That's very impressive." The Overseer's voice was colder than usual and void of any emotion.

"He's finally suitable enough for my granddaughter. I have approved their union."

Yes, Father." Everything was quiet for a moment. "How is the domestic situation faring?"

The general chuckled. "The terrorists have taken a few territories and are now demanding a re-establishment of the states and their governments. Of course, they are also asking for 'equality for all' and the restoration of their precious Constitution. It is completely irrational!" The Overseer agreed.

"And internationally?"

"The North African countries have demanded clarity, and naturally, the monarchy of Panjab has taken their side. They are receiving support from the United East, Korea, and most

Asian nations. France and Germany stand with us, but the rest of Europe is refusing to take a side, those cowards."

"What of Russia?"

The general laughed again, but there was no humor.

"They stand with the savages and Orientals!"

I closed the cupboard and returned to a nearly empty kitchen. My thoughts began to clear when Miss Dae let me go, and as I walked back to the cabins, the darkness seemed a little lighter when paired with the chirping of crickets. All that was left were the fireflies, but they would come a little later.

My bare feet strayed off the dirt path and pressed into the cool, soft grass. It was a second of peace and reflection where I could take the liberty to be free, but even if it was just a moment, it was enough to be thankful for.

Eleven Hours Before Independence Day

CHAPTER FIFTEEN

Patience and Compassion

There was a time when we weren't allowed to drink coffee, but it all changed when Naina's father mistook the cappuccino packets for hot chocolate. How he did that, I have no idea, but it was terrible. I drank it anyway. I didn't want him to feel bad by refusing what I thought at the time was just a different type of hot chocolate, so I finished mine in sips. Ali drank half before he poured the rest into a house plant, and Naina refused to drink it at all. By the time he had realized his mistake, it was too late. Ali and I were running around the house with no end in sight, and Naina and Amrit had joined in, both being extremely energetic by nature. I swore off coffee after that fateful day but, oddly enough, Naina had taken a liking to it. That was what brought her to grab a cup before we continued with the rest of our day.

"Come on, it's just a few blocks down," she urged.

"It's two against one," Ali said.

She groaned before her face lit up.

"I'll buy you a muffin," she offered. He switched sides in a heartbeat and shook Naina's hand to make it official. He shot me an apologetic glance.

"Sorry."

I shrugged. "I guess I could go for a hot chocolate."

Ali laughed.

"What?"

"You're such a kid."

I gaped at him. "I am only two years younger than you."

"Two years can be a lifetime."

"Here we are!" she announced.

Naina saw the sign and walked in without much thought. I nearly followed her in until the white dove on the window caught my eye. It was a warning, but one she had carelessly overlooked. My heart raced as I tried to pull her back outside, but her shirt slipped right through my fingers. I took in a quick breath and did the stupidest thing I could in that situation. I walked right through the door.

Naina was turned with her back to the white-only coffee shop as she laughed. Ali shared her smile until his gaze wandered to take in his surroundings. His face fell instantly.

"Naina." He tried to pull her toward the door, but she slipped away again and continued laughing. The entire shop had gone silent, and its occupants had all turned to stare at us with silent fury. Glass shattered from behind the counter as an employee dropped the cup in his hands.

Naina jumped at the sound and looked around for the first time. She went pale.

A tall, burly man stood from his place by his wife and children and approached us. He stopped inches away from Ali's face with a threatening expression, though none of it echoed in his voice.

"Go." He pushed him forward, but there was no aggression. "Before someone calls the police."

His kindness was the cause for our hesitation and that moment, that split second was all that woman needed.

"How dare you!" She rushed over, but the man stepped in front of us and blocked her path.

"Ma'am, I have this under control."

"Under control! The situation is already at its highest degree." Another man, her husband, joined her.

"Are you defending them?" Disgust laced his tone. I didn't know whether or not we could leave, so I stepped protectively in front of my friends, both of whom were too busy watching the scene to notice.

He glanced back at his children, and his jaw ticked.

"No, of course not."

"Then move," she said. "They need to be taught a lesson." Her husband slipped past the man and got in a punch at Ali before he intervened. The woman nearly broke my nose before I pushed her off. She stumbled back, enraged, and started to make her way forward before she met my gaze. I glared at her and met her in the middle, but my fists remained at my sides.

"I will break your hands if you touch them again." It was too calm to be my voice, but it did the trick. Their steps faltered, from shock or fear, I'm not sure, but it was an empty threat. I didn't know how to break someone's hand, only dislocate it.

"S-Someone c-c-call the police!"

The man pulled me back by my shirt, and his fist connected with my jaw. I fell back into my friends, and they caught me before I could hit the floor.

"There's no need for that." He moved the side of his jacket to reveal his police badge.

"I'll deal with them myself."

He pushed us outside and into an alleyway by the shop. We turned around with collective resolve. We would lose miserably, but we wouldn't go down without a fight. I had already put up my fists when I realized what he was doing. Absolutely nothing. He was standing with his shoulder against the wall, watching us. No hostility or anger suggested that he would follow through, and I didn't know how to feel about that.

We all looked at each other for a tense moment before he spoke.

"That was stupid." He turned to me. "But you've got guts. I can respect that." Ali choked on his own spit, and Naina put her hands through her hair, her eyes wide.

"We're all going to die."

The man frowned at her statement. "No, no. Just stay put for a minute. If I go back too quickly, they'll get suspicious and call my colleagues." We would never come back if they took us away in handcuffs. There would be no trial and nothing left of our existence aside from old photos and forgotten memories, so we did as he said.

The silence was deafening as we waited for what I thought was inevitable, but it never came. He just stood there checking his watch every so often to count down the seconds, and when the time had come, he did raise his fists, but they weren't aimed at us.

"God help me," he whispered.

The man punched the wall until his knuckles split and blood dripped from his skin. It fell to the ground like raindrops when he shook out his hands.

"Wait until I walk through the door and be quick."

We parted ways, and I never saw him again, but I remembered him vividly. His kindness did more than save us that day; it made me question the world I thought I knew. He saved our lives, and I didn't even know his name. There was no thank you, no exchange of favors. He was kind for the sake of it, and that was all I needed to believe in the future Ms. Garcia hoped for.

Ten Hours Before Independence Day

CHAPTER SIXTEEN

Dignity and Prosperity

With the crisis averted, and Naina's sudden lack of appetite, we had nearly decided to go home.

That was until Ali made the case for his forgotten muffin.

"It's just a muffin."

"On the contrary," he replied, "I was owed a muffin, and I will receive one as per our previous agreement." I couldn't help smiling.

"Those are a lot of big words, Veere."

"This is a *serious* conversation," he replied.

Naina scoffed. "And we just had a *serious* encounter with death."

"But we survived." He smiled. "And that's what counts."

"He's got you there, Bhenji." She glared at me, annoyed that I was taking his side. I put my hands up in surrender, and she sighed.

"Fine, let's go." The closest thing to a coffee shop near us was a small German bakery on the corner. The grey circle on its window granted us access. I had never been there before, but it was one of Ali's favorite places to go when he had a dollar to spend.

I offered to order and made my way to the counter while they waited by the door. A boy roughly around my age stepped in front of the register. He was in a pale blue sweater, and his hand clenched the Star of David around his neck as he glanced up.

"Hey, Noah. I didn't know you worked here." He fidgeted with his fingers, and his gaze never met my own.

"It's my father's b-bakery." I ordered and paid.

"H-How ..." He paused for a moment to collect himself before continuing, "How is t-the paper for English g-going?"

"I haven't started it yet."

"I like the t-topic this week."

"Me too. Thanks for the coffee."

"I-It was nice seeing you." He smiled and waved as I left.

I struggled to carry the scolding coffee and hot chocolate without burning my hands, but I made it to the door without too much trouble.

"What took you so long?" I gave Ali his muffin and told them about my conversation.

"Noah? He's in my math class." Naina glanced back at him as we walked out.

"I heard he lost his brother a few months ago when the riots started again."

I burned my tongue and nearly spit out my drink.

"Careful." He laughed. "Where to now?"

"Your house." He nodded, and I smiled, hoping for the best.

We walked through the city's boisterous streets and into the friendly suburbs hidden and secluded from the rest of the world. There was little to worry about in our small, colored neighborhood besides the kids who broke the occasional window playing baseball and the lonely man a few houses down who voiced his pain with anger. It wasn't perfect, but it was ours, so we embraced it.

"I brought food," Ali called into the house as he opened the door and took off his shoes. Leila and Latif rushed down the stairs and nearly tripped over themselves as they ran into us. He split the muffin in two and waited for them to calm down before placing it into their outstretched hands.

They ran off into the living room, and we followed them.

"Surprise!" Amrit yelled at the top of his lungs as he jumped into the hallway and tackled Ali. Naina stumbled into me to avoid them, and everyone ended up sprawled out on the floor.

"You're here!"

"Of course I'm here! I couldn't miss my little brother's big day!" Ali stood up and fixed his hair with a laugh.

"You make it sound like I'm five."

Amrit threw his arm over my shoulder and crushed me with a tight hug as Ali walked into the living room.

Aunt Inaya and Uncle Mihran had taken the day off specifically for this purpose. They wanted to be there when Ali found out where his life would go next, so when he saw them, they were waiting with the letter.

"What is this?" His steps faltered. They stood up and gave him a comforting hug before putting the letter in his hands.

"Open it, son." Aunt Inaya held onto Uncle's hand. "We're here for you, whatever happens."

He looked around at each of us before falling back into the nearest chair, his hands trembling as he held onto the paper that would dictate his future.

"Here goes nothing."

He slit the envelope and opened the letter. We watched in silence as his eyes took in the words on the page. I was hopeful, standing behind everyone else who had subconsciously taken a step forward, with the thought that there was nothing more we could do. The matter had never been in our hands.

Naina, after a few minutes, couldn't wait any longer. She moved forward and took the letter right out of his hands. The tension had reached its peak as she read, her emotions shifting from fear to surprise and then to the one I saw so rarely.

"He got in!" she screamed. Aunt and Uncle started crying, and Leila and Latif, naive to the weight of her words, started jumping up and down because everyone seemed happy, and they wanted to be happy too.

"Congratulations, Veere." He looked up, broken from his thoughts with bright eyes.

"Thanks." He smiled as he pushed back the tears and laughed. Amrit messed up his hair again and joked about how he had worried for no reason.

I watched their reactions quietly. With the doubt gone, I could finally look toward the future. Ali would go to college and work until he made a name for himself. Naina and I would finish what was left of high school and apply, even though the acceptance rates for colored women were close to nonexistent, and move from there. Naina would probably start a restaurant, as she often talked about doing, and I would be left to figure out what I wanted to do and if I had the ability to do it.

It was a small victory. There was no certainty of the future, but Ali had finally gotten his chance, and that was enough to hope for.

"We have to go tell your parents! Look after the twins; we'll be right back." I nodded because no one else was listening. They were too happy to remember the world around them. Ali had started crying, which made Naina cry when she tried to comfort him. The sudden change was enough to startle the twins.

Leila tugged on Ali's pants.

"Why are you crying?" Her voice wavered as tears fell out of her eyes. "Don't cry."

Latif turned to me. "Bhenji?" I crouched down in front of him.

"Why is everyone crying?" he sobbed.

I picked him up and threw him into the air a few times until he laughed.

"Me next!" Leila yelled. I set him down and went in for round two.

"Okay," I said, a little breathless, "no more crying."

Leila rubbed her eyes.

"Can we play?"

"I think that's a great idea." Amrit took her into his arms and ran upstairs with Naina and Ali.

"Don't you want to go?"

Latif shook his head. "I'm hungry."

That's how I found myself struggling to cut apples in the kitchen.

"A man was mean to Abbu today."

"Yeah?" He nodded.

"Why are people so mean to us?"

I picked up a few different colored apple slices and put them on his empty plate before I tried to explain racism to him how my parents had explained it to me.

"What do you notice about the apple slices?"

He frowned for a moment, thinking before his hand shot up.

"The color! They have different colors!"

I nodded. "That's why some people are mean. They don't like that we're a little different."

His frown returned. "But they're not different."

"What?"

He pointed to his plate. "They're all apples. And besides," He turned them so they sat on the peel. "They look the same on the inside. Why does it matter if they don't match?" He jumped out of his seat after he grabbed a few and mumbled under his breath.

"Grown-ups are so weird." I laughed.

"Really?" His cheeks grew pink.

"No?" He rubbed the back of his neck. "Can I go play with Leila now?" The sound of laughter upstairs echoed down into the kitchen.

"Sure." He ran off, and I followed him into the twins' room.

"Please, have mercy!" Ali was on his knees, and Leila, oddly enough, had a plastic sword pointed at him. She narrowed her eyes at her brother.

"No." The sword fell forcefully on his temple.

"Ow!"

"I want to play too!" Latif grabbed a wand from their small bucket of toys and joined his sister as Ali tried to protect himself from their continuous hits.

We were happy, and even though it was just for a second, with no chance of being anything more than a moment in time, I still hoped that it would last forever.

Present Day

CHAPTER SEVENTEEN

Pride and Humility

It was a cool afternoon. Clouds covered the sun, though the rain seemed far away.

Every so often, a light breeze would grace us with its presence, and the silence would be broken.

The Overseer's wife had us working in the backyard today. Apparently, the flowers were too colorful, and she wanted something more elegant, so, of course, she went with white roses. They were difficult to work with and even harder to plant. My arms were covered with cuts from the thorns despite my long sleeves.

Amrit stood up with his hand on his lower back and stretched with a groan.

"You look like more of an old man every day."

He leaned on his shovel. "What makes you say that?"

I shrugged. "The chronic back pain and your long-standing obsession with raisins and cranberry juice."

"Raisins are just like dates," he argued, "just smaller."

"It has nothing to do with the size. They are dried grapes," I said slowly. "And dates are an entirely different fruit."

He scowled at the thought. "I hate grapes."

"That's why it doesn't make any sense."

He picked up a rose bush. "Your hatred for tomatoes is what doesn't make sense. You have no problem with tomato sauce."

"It's a sweet vegetable," I countered.

"Carrots are sweet too, and besides, they're a fruit, not a vegetable."

"Carrots are carrots. They're allowed to be sweet, and tomato is not a fruit."

"I don't agree with that."

"You don't have to."

He offered a hand. "Agree to disagree." I shook it and broke the tension in a heartbeat, but it returned quickly as a familiar voice reached my ears.

"I am not Leonardo, and I will never be anything like you."

The open curtains showed the truth hidden behind the perfect white walls of the mansion. The Overseer picked up a decorative dove and threw it down hard enough that the glass shattered over the marble floor. Elijah's hands shook, but he clenched them before his father could notice.

"You will treat me with respect!" He grabbed his son's shirt and pushed him into the wall.

"I can't do what you've told me," he yelled. His voice was muffled and hard to understand in the quiet. "I can't be the man you want me to be. It's against my nature, Father."

"Your nature? You are a man. You have but one nature."

"I won't do it," he said, steadfast.

"You will. You are the heir to my legacy, and you will learn to uphold it." He let go and stepped away, leaving the boy alone to contemplate the weight of his words.

"Meher." My gaze broke away from the scene.

"Hand me the shears?" I did as my brother asked and continued the task at hand.

The back doors opened, and Elijah walked through them absentmindedly. His eyes fell on me only when I stood to ease my sore knees, and his steps faltered before he stopped. There was a moment of deliberation before he approached me.

"I ..." Elijah started. Amrit threw his shovel to the ground and stood between us.

"What?" His sharpness surprised me, but Elijah took no longer than a few seconds to respond.

"I want to offer a proper apology. I shouldn't have—"

"But you did."

Elijah shook his head. "My father, he—"

"What? He made you?" Amrit's jaw clenched. "And now you suddenly have the courage to approach my sister like nothing happened? Where was that courage when you were with your father? Where was this resolution when he put the whip in your hand?"

Elijah's jaw ticked. "You don't know me."

"I know enough. You're a coward, Elijah Griffin. Your guilt is clawing at your conscience so you came here to get the closure you think will release you from your sins." Elijah's gaze lingered on Amrit before he glanced at me,

109

conflicted, and walked away. Amrit returned to his spot by my side and continued his work as if nothing had happened.

"That was stupid," I said angrily.

"It was," he admitted.

"And completely unnecessary." He pressed down the soil as he planted the last rose bush. He was more serious than I had seen him in a long time, but he refrained from speaking.

"He could have killed you, you idiot," I nearly yelled. I had learned to suppress my anger, but it threatened to crack through the foundation of my composure.

He stopped moving. "I'm sorry."

I turned away with a sigh.

"I can take care of myself, Veere."

"I know," he stood up, "but we're family. We take care of each other."

The words were the only reason I had made it as long as I had. I couldn't do this without them and, as selfish as it was, there was relief in knowing that I wasn't alone. They shared my pain, but they also shared with me the small moments of joy we were blessed enough to have. We laughed together and smiled when it was too painful to do anything else. He was my older brother and now, more than ever, he had taken up the responsibility that came with the title.

The night came and with it, a restlessness. Sleep refused to come, and the throbbing pain in my back made it difficult to relax. My wounds were healing, but there were always new ones. The Overseer had been too busy with the general to do much more than throw a few punches in his spare time, so my most recent had come from the guards. I sat up, and the boards creaked with the shift in weight. I rested my head on my knee as the pain continued to grow.

"Meher?" Naina looked over and sat up beside me.

"Are you okay?" she asked. I smiled even though she couldn't see me.

"Yeah."

"Is there anything I can do?"

"No," I said softly.

She sat with me. In the midst of a dark night, she gave me the only thing she could offer, and it was enough to have her company.

"Do you remember when our parents took us to the park for your birthday? I tripped into a tree and got a bloody nose, but we didn't tell anyone. We didn't want to go back home, and we were having so much fun."

My head fell onto her shoulder as the exhaustion grew to overcome the pain. I wrapped a hand around my ribs and laughed quietly.

"Those were the good old days," I sighed.

She hummed. "How much does it hurt?"

I didn't answer.

"How much?" she repeated.

"Enough."

Her head fell back to rest against the wall as she began to hum. It sent me back home to the nights we would sleep over at her house. She would hum to herself when the clouds roared and lightning cracked through the sky, when we couldn't sleep because the thunder was too loud. Now, there was nothing but silence, and I wondered if I missed the noise.

Everything changed with the funeral. It was hard for her father to handle the three of us by himself, so Ali's house became our new usual rendezvous. My parents were always too busy with work, so it was just the four of us until my brother left for college.

"Is she asleep?" Amrit asked.

"I think so," Naina said as he turned to stare at the ceiling.

"Can't sleep?" Ali asked as he sat up.

"No."

"Well," I sat up properly, "I can't either."

"Anyone up for a walk?" she said out of the blue.

"They'll see us," I whispered.

Naina stood up and stretched. "The guards are probably snoring away, and even if they do see us, they won't do anything. It's not like we're going to run. We have nowhere to go."

Ali snorted. "We could always learn to live in the woods."

I considered it for a second. "We would die from dehydration and exposure."

He snapped his fingers as we walked through the door.

"We could build a treehouse between the branches of a really sturdy tree. We'd have a secure and hidden shelter, and we would be able to live out a childhood dream."

"What about water?"

He brushed off the question. "I'm sure there's a river around here somewhere."

"Disease?" I asked.

"That's a tough one, but hear me out, we'll just dilute whatever's in our system by drinking a lot of water."

"You can drink too much water," Amrit said.

"He's right. It's a thing." Ali stumbled over his sprained ankle, but Naina caught him by the arm before he could fall. She offered to sit by a tree near the cabins, and Ali agreed. The grass was soft under my hands.

It was just us, the four of us against a society that had decided our worth from the moment we were born.

I took in the cold air as we watched the stars.

It was so different here. Back home, I could pretend there was nothing to worry about. I would pretend to be normal, often forgetting there was no real definition of the word. For me, normal was family. It was coming home from school with bruises because the other kids thought it was weird that I wore a dastaar. Normal was reading when there was no one to talk to and living in a fictional world because it was a way to escape the one I woke up to every day. Maybe my normal would finally change, but for that to happen, society would have to change. People would have to change, and that was as probable as the disappearance of the stars. They would always be there, twinkling in the darkness.

Seven Hours Before Independence Day

CHAPTER EIGHTEEN

Home

The next few hours were spent together in Ali's house. Aunt Inaya and Uncle Mihran had invited my parents and Naina's father over for dinner and tea to celebrate Ali's acceptance to university.

Naina was helping Ali's parents in the kitchen, so I was left to put the twins to bed.

"I don't want to go to sleep, Bhenji!"

I sat down on Leila's bed. "What if I tell you a story?"

Latif sighed. "Okay, but it has to be awesome!"

"And funny!"

"I'll try my best." I laughed. I told them the story of a book I had started reading recently, *Frankenstein*, though I took the liberty to make it child friendly.

"Why is Mr. Victor mean to the monster?" Leila asked.

I shrugged.

"I haven't finished the book yet. I'll tell you when I do."

Latif raised his hand suddenly.

"I know! It's because he's different."

"Well, it's a little bit more complex than—"

"The monsters like the green apple."

"He's not gree—"

"You're right," Leila interrupted. "He's different, that's why Mr. Victor doesn't like him." She turned to me.

"Right Bhen?"

I nodded.

"Yeah, now go to sleep, you little monsters."

They laughed when I tickled them and yawned after they had calmed down. I turned off the lights.

"Bhenji?"

"Yeah?"

"Never mind." Latif slid deeper into bed.

"Abbu always tucks us in," Leila said. I tucked them in with a smile and closed the door as I left. The kitchen was filled with conversation and laughter, but my mother's smile was lined with hidden worry, and my father was struggling to hide the confliction in his eyes.

"Are you guys okay?"

"We'll talk after dinner."

"Meher?" Aunt Inaya called for me. "Could you take out the trash? I would ask Ali, but he seems busy." I looked over and held in a laugh when I realized what was happening. Amrit and Uncle Hiresh, Naina's father, were talking to him about his future, and Ali was basically sweating.

"Sure."

I stepped out into the winter air in nothing but a jacket and closed the lid when I was done. I stood there for a second to watch my breath fog up in the air. It was enough to give me comfort. The lights were on in every home as snow fell from the sky, but everyone was inside, so it was peaceful to stand under the stars. I turned to leave before I noticed someone by the door of my house. I moved forward curiously.

"Ms. Garcia?" She turned around, relieved, and walked over to my place on the driveway.

"Did I forget to bring in a book?"

She shook her head, her lips absent of their usual smile.

"No, I just wanted to give you something before I left."

I frowned. "You're leaving? Where are you going?"

"That's not important." She took my hand in hers and I nearly pulled away.

"I-uh-I just took out the trash ..." I paused as my concern for her took priority.

"Did something happen?"

She smiled through her tears. "Everything is going to be okay." She gazed at me for a moment before pulling away, and I watched as her hand went to reach a document hidden in her dark coat. She gave it to me.

"I want you to have this."

I looked through the pages.

"*I have a dream* ..." I read out loud. "What is this?"

"Something I've been saving for a long time. Read it. I'll wait."

"Ms. Garcia—"

"Please, Meher."

I nodded and looked down at the first page. A range of emotions filled me as I read what could be the anthem of equality.

"*Great God a-mighty, We are free at last,*" I whispered as I finished. I met her gaze with too many questions to ask.

"To be judged by the content of our character," she paraphrased. "It's the future I hope for. It's the world I want my son to grow up in. I just wanted you to know that it's possible. They don't teach you history anymore, but people achieved it once. They got rid of segregation, and there was so much more opportunity for colored people and women and anyone with a different religion."

This didn't make any sense.

"It's against the law to protest, and they'd kill us if we spoke against the Charter."

"It was a different time, then." She laughed at herself. "Then? I lived in the time before the war, dear. I've lived in a world where schools weren't segregated and diversity was sought after. Racism was a problem, but we accepted it as something that would change with time." She shook her head. "No one thought that it would amount to this."

"What changed?"

"We elected the wrong people. Everyone was so occupied with the war to realize that the powerful were profiting from it. Children were leaving their families to fight, and anyone left on this side of the border was trying to survive the changing economy. We were struggling to live with the uncertainty that came with war, and they took advantage of us."

"When America lost, everything changed. The shame of losing to the countries in Africa and Asia was too much to handle, so they lashed anyone who looked similar to the people who had defeated them. The Constitution turned into the Charter, and here we are."

"Why are you telling me this?" I asked.

"I might not see you again."

"I don't understand."

"You will, when the time comes." She smiled at me one last time.

"Goodbye."

I watched her leave with the thought that there was nothing I could do. I questioned that decision to this day. I could have asked her to stay for dinner. She would have refused, but I would have insisted and used Ali's acceptance as an excuse. My regrets held no power, but that did nothing to stop them from entering my mind every now and again.

I hid the speech between the assignments stacked on my desk and went back to Ali's to have dinner, the questions surrounding her words fading as we began to eat. It was only fifteen minutes that we chose to spend with each other that day, but we had failed to acknowledge the world in that time, and it had changed.

My father set down his napkin and looked at the other parents before turning to me. I was helping with the dishes.

"Kids, we want to talk to you in the living room when you finish." We glanced at each other as dread seeped into our bones, and sat down on the couch soon after.

"Meher broke your expensive china!"

I looked over at Naina with wide eyes.

"I didn't tell them about the trampled flowers."

Aunt Inaya gasped. "That was you?"

"I didn't do anything!" Amrit chimed in.

"Well, Ali scratched the car!" I said.

"That was an accident!"

"Kids!" I jumped at the harshness of my father's voice. He was never serious, and my mother, well, she never got emotional. That was why I began to worry when I saw her.

"Mama?" She shook her head and covered her mouth with her hand as she leaned into my father.

"It's about your future, Meher," my father started.

"My future?" The very thought of discussing such a thing brought more anxiety than joy, and it was something my father never had the heart to touch on. He knew of my wishes. He knew that I wanted more than I could ever have, so he never discussed what could not be changed.

"You know that we've always wanted what's best for you."

"You're scaring me," I breathed out. "You're not marrying me off, are you?" It was meant to be a joke, but the possibility of it being true was too real to admit. I didn't believe my parents would ever do something so important without my consent, so I gathered the sliver of patience that remained and waited. Amrit leaned forward, worried.

"What's going on?"

"You're not going to be able to go to college here and things are only going to get worse in America. We want you to have the same opportunities as your brother."

"Papa—"

"I have an old friend in Panjab who owes me a favor. The schools there are better than anything you could ever get here, and he's even offered to get you enrolled."

"You're sending her away?" Amrit breathed out. I grabbed his arm as I listened. This was everything I had ever wanted, freedom, opportunity, but something about it unsettled me. There was one thing I had forgotten to consider.

"Papa—"

"He's also offered you a job, son. After you finish college, you'll be going too."

"Papa!" I yelled. Silence reigned again as I looked at my parents. "I can't leave you alone to fend for yourselves."

"Meher—"

"Who's going to take care of you when you get old? Who's going to help you carry the groceries when it's cold or make porridge when you don't feel well if I'm gone? I can't leave you behind."

"You have to." Papa put a hand on the side of my head as my vision blurred. "Go and live your life," he said. "We'll be waiting here when you get back."

"I'm not going to let her go." Amrit's arm was sturdy around my shoulders. "You can't possibly think that she'll be able to focus on school when you're both a billion miles away."

"It's not your choice to make," Papa said plainly.

I covered my face in my hands as I let myself wonder, for the first time in years, what life would be like outside the walls of my current reality. It was terrifying to think that the future could change, and that I would be alone in a new city, but it was not the only thought that occupied my mind. It was the realization that I would be free from the constraints of this society and free to make a life for myself that would be an accumulation of my greatest accomplishments and failings. It would be chaotic, but it would be mine. It was all I had ever wanted, all I never had the heart to ask for, though one question remained. Did I have the courage to follow my hopes and work towards the possibility of achieving my dreams?

"I'll go." I looked at my father and smiled boundlessly. "I'll go," I laughed.

My father embraced me in a warm hug and joined in on my laughter.

"Thank you," I said.

"I'm just happy that I could give you this much."

The sound of a gunshot broke through the mix of emotions that had previously flooded the room and muffled police sirens seeped through the walls before I could hear the echo of our laughter. The door opened and shut, and no one moved until Uncle Hiresh said the only words that would be greater than the news I had just been given.

"They're here. We have to go."

Present Day

CHAPTER NINETEEN

Trust and Compassion

The barn seemed empty without the foal. I had been previously tasked with her care, and now that she was gone, it was different. Everything had gone back to normal, and I had gotten back into the monotonous flow of things, but there was a void with her absence.

I took a bucket of milk into the kitchen and smiled at Miss Dae, her bruises alarming, though not unusual. The general had decided to extend his stay so things had gotten quieter. If there was a crueler man than the Overseer, it was his father. The man who had raised a monster had to be one himself, I suppose, but we were careful.

"Do you need any help?" I asked.

"No, dear. Thank you." I left quietly and stopped in front of the barn where the others were waiting.

"Erasto wants us to start the project by the gate." Amrit said with a sigh.

"The Overseer's wife?" I asked. She loved unnecessary renovation.

"You guessed it."

The same white roses were waiting for us at the entrance, and we began the work that would ultimately take dozens of hours. The sun was forgiving, and the air less humid than it had been for the last couple of days. Ali and Naina left to grab a few things, so I started organizing the supplies with Amrit. The freedom that came with being outside the walls was compelling, but unrealistic. The road in front of the gates would not lead to a better life than the one I currently had. If anything, it would take it away.

I took a shovel and began digging. Amrit and I did most of the hard labor, Ali planted, and Naina did everything in between. Hours passed like this before we encountered an unusual change.

"I will not!" I looked towards the noise, surprised to see a woman a few years older than my brother approaching the gates.

"Miss—" the man began.

"How dare you, Harrison! I will wear what I please." She straightened her loose white button up. "You expect me to wear a dress in this weather?"

"Miss Elizabeth, your father will not appreciate the pants." She glared in his direction.

"Please, return to the car," he urged.

"I prefer to walk."

The man sighed. "Alright, Miss, but the pants?"

"They will stay, Harrison! This was never a problem in England," she muttered. She walked quickly before stopping in front of us.

"White roses?" She sighed. "I will not question my stepmother's ignorance, but at the very least, she should have considered adding some color. The place is already so bland." She walked through the gates with that thought, and we were left alone with the blossoming roses.

"This woman is going to bring a hurricane," Naina laughed.

"Or a Tsunami," Ali snorted.

"A volcanic eruption," Amrit added.

I shrugged.

"That means she's going to change things, and I don't think that's going to happen."

"It might, if she says something that makes the Overseer think about more than himself," Naina offered.

I shook my head.

"She has to change his heart. He has to understand and empathize. If he can't realize the cruelty of his actions and see the world he's created for what it really is, nothing will change."

"Well," Amrit said with a smile, "we could just watch and see what happens."

The rest of the day, like every other, was spent working until the arrival of the moon. We went back to the cabins and ate dinner. I was about to turn in for the night when Erasto asked me to check up on Midnight. I didn't think much of it, but I was alarmed when I saw her restlessness.

"Hey, Midnight." She moved forward when she saw me.

"It must be lonely here now that Hope and Knight are gone. He should be back in a few days, but I'll visit as much as I can," I offered. I knew she couldn't understand me, but she was more human than most of the people here, so it felt natural. I fed her a handful of treats and looked over when I heard someone approaching.

"The nerve of that man!" she muttered to herself, her steps passionate and angry. Elizabeth was in a pair of pajamas with a journal clutched to chest. She faltered when she saw me but continued until she stood right in front of me.

"Elizabeth Griffin." I shook her outstretched hand but made no move to introduce myself.

"Do you mind if I ask you a question?"

I shook my head, unsure.

"Why is it a crime for me to wear pants?" She pointed to her clothes. "They are just pajamas. Pajamas!" she repeated, incredulous. "But my father still believes that a night dress would be more appropriate." She shook her head. "Forgive my forwardness, but he has no problem with you and your friend wearing pants." My mouth went dry. "Why is that?" she asked.

"He doesn't know that we're women, and I would appreciate if it can stay that way." I reached over and rubbed the side of Midnight's neck, and she rested her head on my shoulder.

"You should be proud of who you are," she said.

I pulled away. "I am doing what I have to."

Elizabeth frowned, confused.

"You may work for my father, but he is not as bad as he seems." She paused.

"Regardless, I will honor your decision." She sat down on a hay barrel and began writing in her journal. I took the moment to get some more treats for Midnight, but as soon as I was gone, she started kicking the gate of her stall.

"Miss?" Elizabeth called for me, alarmed. Midnight's aggression was aimed towards the newcomer, but I did nothing to hurry, knowing that she would calm when she saw me again.

"Be nice," I said as I came to stand in front of her stall again. She blew air into my face and relaxed as I fed her. She, like me, found comfort in food. Treats eased her anxiety. The only food that could do that for me was anything my mother decided to make for dinner after a long day.

"Miss?" I turned to look at Elizabeth and the pen in her hand tapped softly against the paper as she spoke.

"Do you read?" she asked.

"I used to."

"Miss Elizabeth? Oh, thank heavens!" Harrison entered the barn, relieved. His gaze lingered on me before it fell, and there was an unusual emotion in his eyes. If he didn't know about the Bonded before, he certainly did now.

"It's late," he started. "Your father is calling for you."

She sighed. "Tell him that I am with my sister's horse."

He frowned. "You have never been one to ride, Miss Elizabeth."

"You're right. I need something more ... believable." She stood up and paced a few times. "Tell my father that the night air is good for my skin. If it has to do with beauty, he will not bother me."

"Alright, but be back soon, Miss."

She smiled. "I will surely try."

He shook his head as he left.

"Do you mind if I stay?" she asked. I pulled away from Midnight.

"No."

She continued writing as I stood there. Exhaustion lingered in my bones, but I didn't move until I was sure Midnight would be okay for the rest of the night. When the time came, I said a quick goodbye.

"I should get going."

Elizabeth glanced up briefly. "Goodnight."

I spotted Naina by the door and walked with her as we went back to the cabin.

"Meher?" I hummed.

"Don't get comfortable with them," she said.

"I won't."

"They'll move on, but we'll be left to live with the consequences of their curiosity." She stopped and turned to face me. "Okay?" she asked quietly.

"Yeah, Bhen."

She pulled me in for a hug. "I just don't want you to get hurt."

I laughed into her shoulder.

"What?" She pulled away.

"You're just like my mother," I said. I continued down the path and turned around when I didn't hear her beside me.

"Coming?" I asked. She put her arm around my neck and pulled my face into her collarbone, holding me there until she stopped laughing. I ripped away and rubbed the back of my neck.

"What was that for?"

She shrugged. "I haven't done it in a while."

I smiled with her. Every now and again, Naina's old personality shone through, and it sent me back to the days we would spend together. Ali and I were always reading and Amrit had taken to video games at a young age, but Naina had a passion for baking and pranks. She would sneak up on me when I wasn't paying attention and push me out of my seat or scare me so that I would jump out of it myself. She made us cookies when we were upset or when she wanted to apologize but couldn't find the words. It was in moments like this that I saw glimpses of the old Naina. She was still there, I was sure, hidden under the scars.

Six Hours Until Independence Day

CHAPTER TWENTY

Cruelty and Kindness

The sound of police sirens filled my ears as different cars and buses filed into the neighborhood. It was an unusual sight, but the adults looked like they knew what they were doing, so I trusted my parents to guide us.

"It's just a relocation. We need to stay calm."

"What?"

"We need to go."

Aunt Inaya ran upstairs to wake up the twins, and everyone left through the back door to go home. They didn't see us. We were lucky that they were too preoccupied with the houses further down the street to notice.

"Pack a bag. Only essentials, do you understand?"

"Mama—"

"Now, kids. I will explain everything," she promised, "just not right now." I nodded and did as she said. My heart pounded in anticipation as I ran around my room and grabbed everything that seemed important. I slung the bag over my shoulder and took one last look at the place I knew I would never see again. I missed it now, my old bed and my desk filled with papers.

"Meher!"

"Coming!" My parents were waiting by the door. My mother crouched down and put her hands on my cheeks as I put on my shoes.

"They're going to take you away, but they won't kill you." My father got down beside her and put his hand on the side of Amrit's head. My brother stopped moving beside me to stare at my father with the love he never showed for him. Their relationship had always been less affectionate, but at that moment, my father proved that he loved him as much as he loved me.

"Things will be different, and you'll have to adapt, alright sweetheart? Just don't forget who you are." They hugged each of us and pulled away as the noises outside got louder.

"You aren't coming with us?" Amrit asked.

My father shook his head. "They'll separate us." His hand stayed on my shoulder while the other went to my cheek. He kissed my forehead before pulling away and turning to us both.

"We're so proud of you." They watched us tenderly in the seconds before the door broke down, before they ripped us apart and dragged me and my brother into a separate bus. I took a seat in the back across from Ali and Naina, and my head fell forward into my shaking hands. It was funny how despite everything, *everything*, the only thing that I could think of was the last thing they said.

We're proud of you.

My smile disappeared as screams began to accompany the rough yelling. Men in uniforms, soldiers, pushed people into the buses forcefully, and fear filled the air. I jumped when a body hit the floor, and in seconds, one gunshot turned into dozens. I did the only thing I could. I closed my eyes, waiting as my ears rang in the cold of an early December morning, and tried to make sense of the situation.

A colored woman sat down in the seat next to me before Amrit could. Her lips fell into a frown when she saw who I was, or what I was, I suppose. She made no move to say what I already knew. We were colored. We were different, but we were not the same. The Aryans saw us all as one thing, but we had created factions within ourselves. People stayed with their own, black with black, brown with brown. A few, like the owners of the German bakery, accepted the term colored as something that defined everyone who didn't fit the government's description of a perfect citizen. We had separated ourselves because we, like those above us, had started believing that one color and religion was better than the others. We had made their mistake.

The people were silenced before the bus pulled out of the neighborhood. There were no more stops and no sound aside from the joyous voices of the men who had taken us. Ali and Naina waved to make sure that I was okay, and I smiled, despite myself, to offer them the assurance that I couldn't give myself. I found Amrit seated a few seats ahead and only then was I able to breathe.

My head rested against the window as the lights passed. I watched the world until we left the city and the anxiety

131

previously built up in my chest began to wane as people fell asleep around me. I crossed my arms over my chest and closed my eyes. I couldn't sleep, but it was easier to let my mind wander this way.

"Switch with me," the woman beside me spoke.

"They might see us," another answered.

"It's dark, and I don't want to sit next to this Terror." Disgust laced her tone. I heard a sigh before the other woman agreed.

"Hello." I looked over. The woman's bright blouse complimented her dark skin and her smile reminded me of a sunflower.

"Hi," I replied.

"I'm Nava." She offered a hand, and I shook it.

"Meher."

She leaned back against her seat. "I think we have biology together."

"With Mr. Tanaka?" I asked.

She nodded.

"Then I think we do."

She stretched out her arms with a quiet laugh. "At least we don't have to turn in the project. I was having a lot of trouble with my bean plants. They just refused to grow!" she whispered.

"Did you try to use a humidifier? The air gets really dry in the winter."

"That's not a bad idea. I'll try that when this whole thing blows over." I paused for a moment to consider my question before voicing it.

"How can you be so carefree?"

She shrugged. "I'm just trying to make the best of a bad situation. Crying won't help anyone, and fear just fuels their egos. We can't do anything but play it smart and hope for the best." She looked over with bright eyes. "And besides, I like smiling."

I let my head fall back as my growing headache began to worsen.

"Why bean plants?" I asked.

"I thought they would be easy to grow. It was either that or pumpkins, and I hate pumpkins. What did you choose?"

"Tomatoes. I don't particularly care for them, but my brother loves them." I rubbed my eyes. "I forgot to water them yesterday."

"I'm sure they'll be fine," she said passively.

"I hope so. I put good work into those tomatoes. There's a designated spot for them in my basement, and I fixed up these fluorescent lights to put on the ceiling so they would get enough light."

"You're very passionate about your tomatoes." I laughed a little.

"I guess so."

The streetlights returned as we entered a nearby town, but the streets remained barren and empty of life. There were hundreds of worn shoes strung over the power lines.

"Those are all the people that haven't come back," she said. I touched the window before letting my palm rest against the cool glass.

"There are so many."

"Those are only the ones in this town. The cops will take them down before lunch tomorrow, and they'll be forgotten again. It's the same story, just with a different person, a different alley."

"A different family," I said.

"Did you lose someone?" she asked.

"Yeah." We all had.

"I did too, a few years ago."

She yawned after a few minutes and closed her eyes.

"Goodnight." I smiled softly as her head fell on my shoulder.

"Goodnight."

Ali had fallen asleep, but Naina was squinting in my direction. I waved and gave her a thumbs up that said I'm okay. My smile fell when she looked away, and I returned again to my place looking out the window. I took a small breath and closed my eyes.

I'm okay.

Independence Day

CHAPTER TWENTY-ONE

Loneliness and Nostalgia

It was still dark when the bus stopped. They moved us out into the open, and we waited silently for what would come next. Some were tired and others too afraid to talk, but it all led to the same thing. They locked us in an empty room with a single flickering lightbulb as the only source of light and heat. People huddled together for warmth and whispered quietly to fill the silence.

"Where are the twins?" I asked.

"With Abbu and Ammi," Ali said as I pushed my sleeves over my trembling hands.

Naina burst out laughing. I jumped at the sound, and my wide eyes shot up to meet Ali's, but he just shrugged and moved away from her a little.

"This is just like when you locked us out of the house last year. Our parents were at that convention, and you were in charge!" Ali pulled up his hoodie to cover his ears.

"I told you to leave the door open!" he whispered.

"It was snowing!"

"No, it wasn't."

"It was," she assured. She turned to me.

"Right, Meher?" I sighed at the devastating memory.

"I dropped my book in the snow, remember?"

His eyes lit up with realization. "That's right."

A fist slammed against the door as noise returned to the room, and it was enough to bring back the silence that had only just left. Amrit leaned into me protectively as a harsh voice resonated through the walls.

"Quiet!"

Naina rubbed her arms, more annoyed at the situation than anything else. She had yet to understand the gravity of our circumstances, and a part of me believed she was still in shock, despite her normal behavior.

"What's his problem?" Ali said as he pulled his knees up to his chest.

"What is wrong with you!" Naina whispered. "It's freezing, and you're wearing the thinnest hoodie I have ever seen!"

"I forgot my coat, okay? It's an honest mistake."

She hit him over the head.

"It's been snowing for the past two weeks."

He gave her his signature lopsided smile. "Sorry?"

She huffed. "You're a grown man. I'm not always going to be there to take care of you." His smile fell and he glanced at the three of us, dejected.

"Don't say that."

I laughed. "As if we'd ever leave you alone. Who else would be tall enough to grab the cookies Mama keeps on the top shelf? We would have to find ourselves another giant when Amrit leaves again for college."

"I'm not that tall," my brother argued.

"Are you calling us short?"

He laughed. "Yes."

I pulled his ear until he apologized, and when I let go, he rubbed the red skin.

"That hurt."

I unzipped my coat and offered it to Ali. He shook his head.

"Take it," I pressed.

"You'll get cold." I threw it at him, and he let it hit his face.

"I have this," I tugged at my thick sweatshirt. "You don't."

"Thank you." He pulled it on. It was a tight squeeze, but he managed to get it to fit. Amrit held in a laugh.

"What?" Ali asked.

"Oh, nothing. The neon blue really suits you."

He smiled. "It's really my color."

A man a few feet away from me stood up and pulled away from the arm keeping him down. He shook his head, terrified.

"I can't do this. They're going to kill us. I have to get out of here!"

He rushed toward the door and threw it open before a ringing filled my ears. Blood splattered over the walls and people as we watched in horror.

The door slammed closed, and we were left to consider the consequences of our actions. I took in a deep breath as my eyes glazed over. Amrit grabbed my arm and pulled me closer.

"It'll be okay." He wrapped his arms around my shoulders.

"He didn't deserve to die," I said.

"I know."

I didn't cry. I couldn't bring myself to be so vulnerable.

"What are they going to do?" Ali's voice was distant, and his eyes were still stuck on the man lying dead on the floor before he closed them. I pulled away from Amrit as my thoughts went back to a conversation that had taken place recently. It was one that had remained in the back of my mind.

"They're going to separate us," I said.

"What?" Amrit asked.

"I think," I added. "Noah found this book in his attic a few months ago. Ms. Garcia does restorations, so we had her take a look at it, and it's really old. Noah thinks it was his great-great great-grandfather's, but the story is really similar to our situation. They took him from his home and put him into a labor camp."

"Is that where they're taking us?" Ali asked.

"I don't know."

Naina crossed her arms over her chest. "That can't happen. They can't separate us."

"What's the plan?" Ali asked.

I shrugged.

"I don't know. Stay together?"

"We'll figure it out." Amrit's words were comforting.

I let out a shaky breath as my body trembled in the passing hours. I fell asleep with my head on Naina's shoulder and woke up only when the door opened again. I shook the others awake.

"Get out!" The soldier stepped away as we filled the courtyard.

"Two lines! Men on the right, women to the left!" I grabbed Naina's arm and pulled her to the right. She pushed her hair into her dark beanie as the two lines were divided into four groups.

"Age?" The soldier asked.

"Fourteen." He pushed the boy toward the fourth group before Ali moved forward.

"Age?"

"Eighteen." He was sent to the third group. My brother was next.

"Twenty-one." He followed Ali.

"Age?" I stepped on Naina's foot before I spoke.

"Eighteen."

I walked toward the third group, relieved that Naina had understood when she joined us.

It didn't long for the lines to dissolve. The men lined up the first and fourth groups against the wall as the sun rose.

The morning began with an echo of gunshots.

Bodies fell one by one, and silence reigned again. The people around me were terrified, but I couldn't bring myself to share in the feeling. I was angry. It was slight, and I knew there was nothing that I could do, but I was angry. There was no humanity, no empathy. They saw us by our differences and nothing else. To them, we were a blotch of color on their perfect white nation that needed to be washed away in blood.

I stepped forward subconsciously and stopped only when Amrit pulled me back, effectively taking me out of my trance. A few of the younger men started disposing the bodies, and we were left to stand and watch. We sat down after a few quiet minutes and continued to wait. There were more rooms filled with other people and slowly, they were let out and either moved to the side or executed. The pile of bodies grew before it diminished, and by the time the bloody snow had soaked through my pants, I could barely feel the cold anymore. My ears were filled with a constant ringing, and there was no emotion left that I could express. I was surrounded by death, and it was colder than any winter I had ever experienced.

God, give me strength.

"No!" A man tore the child from the woman's arms and tossed him to the side before moving on.

"I'm doing you a favor," he assured the black woman. "That thing, your son, is going to grow up to be a thief." He turned to the woman in a hijab. "Yours is going to be a killer and yours," he crouched down in front of the Mexican woman, "is going to ruin hundreds of innocent lives by offering them a way to get high."

The women were on their knees, but there was no grief or fear in their expressions.

"Give back our children," she said slowly, the fury in her eyes speaking volumes, "or I will burn your world to the ground."

He laughed through his fear and waved at the guards.

"It's not my problem," he brushed off as he walked away. They were the last to join our group.

"The general's son requested twelve of the best Bonded," one said, his dark hair sparkling with sprinkles of snow.

"Son?" The soldier laughed. "You mean the man who couldn't keep his family?" He frowned in confusion, so the other continued.

"His sister-in-law thought that he wasn't fit to raise three children on his own, so she took his eldest daughter and his only son. It's a disgrace. The man couldn't even stand up to a woman." They laughed together.

"You're welcome to pick and choose, but it's a waste of your time." He crossed his arms.

"You could always ask for volunteers," he said with a laugh.

"Whatever you say, Thomas."

The buses came again an hour later, and they did ask for volunteers. We stood apart and became four of the twelve who would be sent to live under the general's son. We had found a way to stay together, so we would go down that path, even if it led to more pain. The seats were nearly empty, but everyone moved to the back, and with that, the drive began.

Present Day

CHAPTER TWENTY-TWO

Tragedy and Grief

A storm brewed above. It thundered every so often, warning of what was to come as the wind picked up. I washed the dirt from my hands and went into the kitchen, knowing that when it started to rain, we would be expected to work inside.

"Good afternoon," I said. Miss Dae smiled when she saw me.

"Ah, there you are! I haven't seen you all week. What have you been up to?" I helped her make sandwiches. The Overseer and his family had eaten so now, we could too.

"Work," I said. I was about to take a bite when she slapped the bread out of my hand.

"Don't you try that with me, dear." I shook out my hand with a slight frown.

"This is definitely going to bruise."

She laughed. "If it's anything like last time, I'm sure it will." She gave me a sandwich when we had finished and pushed me toward the door.

"The Overseer has given us the rest of the day off. His daughter is getting engaged."

I picked up an apple. "Can I—"

She looked around before nodding. "Yes. Now, go on, child." Miss Dae ushered me out the door.

"Thank you." I smiled as I walked out. The fields were empty. Everyone and everything had been moved inside, so I was alone. I went to the barn to find that Midnight was outside and with a rider. The man was calm, but he wasn't picking up on her cues. He didn't listen.

"This one is rather disobedient." He said as he tried to push her forward, but she refused and kicked the ground. He whipped her, and I looked away, ashamed that like always, I could do nothing.

"Move!" he demanded.

"Leo—" Willow started.

"Do not distract me. Move, you beast!" Midnight started trotting, but it wasn't long before I heard a body hit the ground. I hid the apple in a nearby stall in hopes of slipping out before anyone could see me, but my attempts were useless. Within seconds, Midnight jumped the fence to meet me in the barn. She huffed when she saw me and calmed down. I moved her into her stall and was about to leave when the man from before approached her.

"She is my horse," Willow said. She hid her trembling hands behind her back.

"You are my woman." She blushed and watched as he walked up to her and stopped only when their faces were mere inches apart. He didn't move until she looked away.

"The horse needs to be punished. Bring her out, Bonded." I did as he said and stepped away, flinching when he whipped her.

"Leonardo, stop. Please," Willow begged. Midnight shifted and was about to run away when he told me to keep her still. I didn't move.

"Bonded," he warned. "Do as I say, or you will be punished in the beast's place." Oddly enough, his words were enough to give me relief. Midnight would be okay.

"Willow, take it to the stall." She smiled and took her by the reins.

"Thank you!" she said. He gave her a small smile.

"Anything for you, my love."

He waited until Midnight was safe inside her stall to throw aside the whip and grab me by my shirt. His fist met the side of my jaw and continued with my face until he threw me aside to shake out his hand. I got up and spit out whatever blood was in my mouth as he pushed back the hair that had fallen over his blue eyes.

"If you beg for forgiveness, I might consider being merciful," he said calmly. I stayed quiet.

He kicked me before I could get up to my feet, and the action was enough to leave me wheezing on the ground. Willow pulled his arm.

"Leo, please."

"What did I tell you about interrupting me?" She looked away as her hands moved to dry her cheeks.

"I'm sorry," she whispered.

He sighed. "Alright, let's go. I'm famished." Willow put her hand on his elbow and leaned into him as they left. Midnight kicked her stall as they passed, but he did nothing but glare at her. The action was useless despite its efforts. Midnight had never been fearful, and she would remain as such.

I stood up after my breathing had returned to normal and approached the mare. I brought out the apple and fed it to her, my elbows leaning on the door as I waited for her to finish.

I gave her a small pat as it started to drizzle and left to wash off the blood that covered my face. The water was ice cold, and it left my hands shaking as I entered the cabin. The people inside were more boisterous than usual, and an aura of joy seemed to resonate in the air. I sat down near Amrit and a sleeping Naina. Ali sat in the corner, his eyes pink and emptier than I had seen them in a long time.

"What happened?" I asked. Ali let his head rest on his knee as tears fell from his closed eyes.

"Dalmar's gone," Amrit answered "They killed him and took him away. I ... I tried—"

"It's not your fault," I said softly.

Ali let out a shaky breath before he spoke. "What number?"

"One hundred forty-three. We can do it tonight," I offered.

He nodded. "Naina—"

"Don't worry about it, Veere. I'll tell her." He curled up in the corner and grieved as Amrit stared at the wooden boards under him. I sat beside him, and it was enough to let him know that he wasn't alone.

A man had died today, a son, a brother, a friend, and though I didn't know him as well as my brothers had, there was still a sadness that lingered at the thought of another death. One hundred and forty-three had died before him, and many more would follow in the coming months. It didn't make any sense to me. Yesterday, he was laughing with Erasto, his father. This morning, he was teaching a few of the others an old dance he had learned as a child, but now, he was gone, and we would never see him again.

We waited until the sun had fallen to slip away to the back of the cabin. The wet grass and soft soil caught on my feet as we stood to pray for him, and when we finished, Ali carved his name into the back of the cabin.

"What are you thankful for?" Naina asked.

Ali glanced over at her and shook his head. "No."

"Five things," she said. "What are five things you're thankful for?"

He let out a shaky breath.

"I'm grateful for the time I got to spend with him." He paused to collect himself before he continued, "I'm glad that I didn't lose any of you."

"Three more."

He nodded. "I'm thankful for the day off and the rain and... and—" His voice broke, and he shook his head. Naina hugged him.

"I just don't want you to forget that there's a lot left to live for."

He cried into her shoulder as the rain began again, but no one moved. We just stood there, soaking wet as we mourned the loss of a friend.

Present Day

CHAPTER TWENTY-THREE

Ignorance and Belief

The Overseer had planned a ball in honor of his daughter's recent engagement. We were tasked with the preparation and maintenance of the evening, which meant that we would clean and set up the decorations while the others made dinner. We would leave as soon as the guests began to arrive, so the evening would be ours. Until then, if he saw us slacking, it was straight to a cell.

I slipped into the kitchen to wash my hands.

"Where's the rest of the flour?"

The girl beside Miss Dae shrugged as I dried my hands.

"I can go get some," I offered.

She smiled in relief. "Thank you, dear."

The storeroom, I liked to believe, was one of Regina's many hobbies. It was one of the few things that she could control, and it was always in pristine condition. Every bag was kept in a specific place because it had a specific purpose, a specific value. It was more value than she had ever given to the slaves.

I found the flour and stopped moving as a quiet noise reached my ears. I turned towards it.

"Hello?" I called out.

"Hi." *Yua?* She wiped away the tears on her cheeks and looked away. I turned back and picked up the flour, hesitating for only a moment as I moved toward the door.

"Midnight is in her stall if you want some company."

"She isn't particularly fond of me."

"Give her an apple, and she'll warm up to you." I said as I turned the handle.

"Thank you." I glanced back as I walked through the door, my mind stuck on the girl I hardly knew. I turned the corner and nearly ran into two people running toward the stairs.

Willow laughed, the dresses in her arms mirroring those in Elizabeth's. She was glowing, but her sister held with her a hesitation, a caution that mirrored that of a person meeting a stranger. Willow stopped when she saw me, and held up her hand to show me the ring.

"I'm getting engaged!"

"Congratulations." I smiled, but it faltered when she looked away. I was nothing more than an acquaintance, but I knew men like Leonardo. She would realize too late if she realized at all.

"Oh, I almost forgot to introduce you. This is my sister. Elizabeth, this is my friend." We shared a glance.

"Look at my dress!" She showed me the sunflower yellow dress, and the color was enough to bring back the memories of a friend.

"It's beautiful," I said. Her smile grew.

"I'll see you at the party!" She ran upstairs with her sister. I took a second to make sure that no one had seen the interaction before leaving to give Miss Dae her requested bag of flour.

"Oh, dear," she said. She pointed to the trail of flour that had leaked from the bag with a heavy sigh. I grabbed a broom and started cleaning when the doors opened. A man was pushed in, one I quickly recognized.

"Do you know how expensive these shoes are?" Leonardo kicked Amrit in the chest.

"They're worth more than all of you savages combined." The two men that had accompanied him grabbed my brother by the arms and brought him up to his knees. His breathing was heavy and inconsistent, too painful to be healthy. There were new bruises covering his skin, and the blood from his healing wounds soaked through his shirt as he looked up to meet the man's gaze.

"Now, who is going to pay for them?" He pulled Amrit up by his shirt.

"I think they're making raspberry tarts." Willow and Elizabeth entered the room nonchalantly, but their steps halted as they took in the scene. Leonardo threw my brother down and kicked him again.

"Leo!" He looked over, bored, before raising his foot again. Elizabeth stood in front of him and pushed him back.

"Show some respect," she demanded.

"Respect?" He laughed. "Why would I do that? They're not worthy of my respect."

"Not worthy? You are more hot-headed than I remember," she said. Willow intervened.

"Leo, please stop." She was on the verge of tears, but Elizabeth was just beginning. "They are people, Leonardo, not punching bags! You cannot treat them however you please just because they work for my father."

He looked between the two, amused.

"You really don't know." He laughed. "You'll find out soon enough. That will certainly be entertaining." Leonardo stepped forward, and Elizabeth followed him.

"Leave him be." Leonardo's smile fell at her words.

"You cannot command me, woman." He tried again to move toward my brother, but again, she stood in his way. His jaw ticked, and he tried to back her into the wall, but she refused to move, so he resorted to the only thing he thought would help him regain the control he had lost.

"Move."

"No."

His face contorted with rage. She had done more than voice her opinions. She had defied him, and that was unacceptable. He raised his arm and backhanded her with enough force to make her stumble. She turned to him with wide eyes.

"How dare you!" she yelled. Willow stood between them in tears. Elizabeth faltered at the sight of her sister, but Leonardo did not.

She pulled Elizabeth's arm. "Let's go."

"Willow—"

"Please," she begged. "Pull away. He will not." She gave in.

"Alright."

Leonardo picked up a vase as soon as they left and threw it down before he rushed through the door. I waited until the room was clear to help Amrit to the cabin and hit him over the head.

"What was that for," he groaned. I stayed quiet as my worry grew quickly into anger. We were careful. Aside from the customary obedience beating the Overseer gave us, there was no other reason to get hurt, but he did. He wasn't careful, and people who weren't careful, well, they didn't make it.

He lifted his head up to look at me as I sat across from him.

"I'll be more careful next time," he promised.

My jaw clenched.

"And what if there is no next time?" He pushed himself up to sit.

"I don't know," he whispered, "but he got what was coming to him."

"You're an idiot," I seethed.

My silence returned. I sat with him until the quiet got too much to bear and left to return to my work. There was little to do, but it took up whatever time was left. Soon enough, the first guest had arrived, and we were ordered to leave, but I didn't return to the cabin. Instead, I sat under a tree near the barn to watch the sunset. It wasn't as beautiful when I watched it alone. The evening chill seeped into my bones as the moon rose to glow with the stars. The wind rustled the leaves above and shifted the grass around me.

"Do you mind if I join you?" Amrit sat down next to me and looked over every so often to see if my expression had changed.

"I'm sorry," he said.

"Something could have happened to you."

"I know. I'm sorry," he repeated. Silence stretched between us until he looked over with a smile. "Naina was worried that you got lost."

"Getting to the cabin?"

He nodded, and I shared a smile.

We laughed together, with the tension now broken, and my anger long forgotten. He leaned against the tree, and its bark caught on his shirt as he looked up at the stars. His expression grew solemn.

"You shouldn't have to worry about me, little sister. I'll be more careful."

"Promise?"

He nodded and brought his pinkie forward.

"Promise."

A twig broke somewhere behind me.

"It looks like the two of you have made up." Naina sat down next to me with a yawn and leaned onto my shoulder. Ali sat down behind her.

"Are we watching the stars? I know that one." Ali said as he pointed to the sky and traced the stars.

"That's the Ursa Major."

We spent the rest of the hour trying to find the other constellations, and the world seemed a little smaller than before. We all lived under the same sky, watched the same stars. We would live and die on the same soil that nurtured the world, but we were too stubborn to admit it. Death was a lifetime away, and life wasn't good enough. Someone could have the world and still not be satisfied when the stars were still out of reach, though they were never meant to be captured. But I had no use for the stars when everything I needed was right here.

Present Day

CHAPTER TWENTY-FOUR

Life

Sleep came late to me that night. Ali was the first to go, and Amrit stayed with me until he couldn't keep his eyes open anymore. I told him to leave with an unspoken indication that I would follow soon after. It didn't end up that way, but it gave him enough reassurance to leave me by myself. I stayed under that tree for nearly an hour more into the night, my thoughts relentless. My time here seemed like a lifetime, but I could do nothing but hope that it wouldn't last much longer. I wanted to go home, and that longing was enough to bring the loneliness that scarcely bothered me these days. Still, it came, and refused to go.

"You missed the engagement." His voice was loud in the darkness.

"I will not attend something I do not support, Elijah. Does Father know?"

"I'm not sure. Grandfather approved the union." Elizabeth sighed.

"And, of course, Father agreed."

"He has never been one to defy our dear grandfather," he said.

"His fear for the man is something I will never understand." The gravel crunched under their feet.

"How are you? I've heard Father has been rather demanding."

"I will never live up to his expectations unless I change. I might," he said. "It's so much easier to give in."

She laughed.

"That makes two of us."

Their voices faded until they were nothing more than whispers, and I waited until I could no longer hear them to make the short journey to the cabin, the loneliness still lingering.

"How long?" *Erasto?*

"One month," a man replied, his voice unknown to me. He was not someone from here.

"That's too long."

"It's the best I can do. There are others that still need to be liberated."

"The general is scheduled to leave in three weeks. They moved up the wedding."

The man thought over his words.

"That changes things."

"Three weeks," Erasto offered, "and my people will stand with you."

"I'll send it forward."

The two parted ways, but the man, I realized, didn't move more than a few steps away. Erasto walked right past me, and the cabin blocked whatever moonlight would have told him of my presence.

156

"Who's there?" the man asked.

"No one important." His golden cross glinted against his otherwise dark form as I stepped into the light. My feet led me closer to the cabin, but I remained cautious.

"Have we met before?" I glanced at the Aryan man and shook my head. I had never seen him before, at least, not that I remembered.

"No."

I stepped through the door after he moved away and began walking towards the bright mansion.

The rest of the night passed normally. There were no more strangers and no more secrets, nothing that would warrant curiosity. The morning came similarly and soon enough, night had fallen again. Another day had passed in dull monotony. It was another day lost and forgotten in the repetition of what I had come to know as my daily life. Even this had become its own type of normal. Every day would be filled with hard labor and every week accompanied with a few beatings. The months brought with them the change of the seasons, and the years held the promise of another life. I had survived one year, what was one more? If only I knew how long it had truly been. Time passed differently for me. There was nothing to look forward to and nothing to prepare for aside from the distant hope that something would change.

I stared at my reflection in the water for a moment before my lips fell into a frown. I looked away and washed my hands.

I didn't know how much time had passed, only that I looked older now and more like my mother. The very thought of her was enough to bring the nostalgia of the beautiful life I had lived before. It was a life with my family, a perfect life.

"That's a weird *thing* that happened yesterday." I nodded at Ali.

"I just don't know what to think about the man Erasto met by the cabin."

Naina hit my arm aggressively, and Ali shushed me. Amrit did nothing but laugh.

"You don't know who that was! It could be someone dangerous," she said.

"What if Erasto is in the CIA? Now he has to kill you because you know too much!" Ali nearly yelled.

"There is no CIA anymore," my brother countered.

"He could be with the White Service. You never know," Naina warned. I rubbed my arm as the skin turned red under my sleeves.

They pulled me to the side of the barn, talking in hushed whispers despite the emptiness that clung to the place. We were the only ones here.

"It's clear," Naina said with a thumbs up.

Amrit leaned against the wood. "Liberation, huh?"

I shrugged.

"It could mean anything. I don't think we should get our hopes up again."

"I don't even think we should be talking about this. What if someone hears us?" Naina whispered.

"She's got a point."

"Nobody's here!" Amrit said.

"Okay, sorry," Naina said half-heartedly. I quickly returned to the topic at hand. "So, what do we make of it? I don't want to believe in something that could never come."

"Better to believe in something than nothing at all," Naina offered.

"I know," I said, "but we don't know what's going on outside the white picket fence of the estate. We could live our entire lives here without any chance to find something else."

"I would rather die."

It was sudden, but Amrit's eyes grew shadowed, and his smile had gone. His words held with them the weight of my entire world, but they were ones I agreed with completely. This was not a life worth living. Still, we tried for ourselves and if not that, then for each other. Hope was the only thing driving us, and if that disappeared, there was nothing left to live for.

"We should go," he suggested.

"I'm going to make sure Midnight's okay. I'll be right there."

My brother's smile returned. "I get it."

"What?"

"Oh, it's nothing, just that I'm being replaced by a horse."

I laughed and shook my head. "No one can replace you, Veere. Who else is going to get the cookies off the top shelf when we get home?"

His gaze softened with his smile. He looked so much like our father at that moment, so kind and comforting. His jaw was sharper and more defined, but he hadn't changed at all. He was still the boy who hated grapes and green beans, the kid would do anything to make me laugh when I didn't have the heart to. He was still my brother.

We had changed so much, but I hadn't noticed, because to me, they would always be my family. They would always be the little kids who pushed me on the swings and carried my library books when I had too many. They were the only people in my life who I loved more than the moon and the stars and the books I never let go.

I made my way to Midnight's stall, hoping to make the journey quick, but an unexpected visitor had sat down in her usual place with the journal that never seemed to leave her side.

"I was hoping to find you here," she said.

I gave her no indication that I had heard her.

"You didn't go to the engagement party."

I frowned but maintained my silence.

"Did you know about Leonardo?"

"I did."

"Why didn't you say anything?"

"I didn't have anything to say."

"You are her friend."

"And you are her sister. Your word will always be worth more than mine."

She shook her head as I left to wash my hands and followed me.

"Willow will not listen to me."

"She will," I said as the gravel pressed into my bare feet. "Have you tried talking to her?"

She looked away. "No."

"Then how do you know?"

Elizabeth straightened her dress.

"She follows my father. She would not disobey him."

"If that's true, then there is nothing either of us can do."

She gaped at me before walking away. She was in a dilemma, seeking someone to blame because she had yet to realize that she had any power to speak in the matter at all.

I cared for Willow the way that I cared for a distant friend. I wished the best for her, but it wasn't my place to speak on matters that didn't concern me. I wouldn't share the heavy weight on her shoulders because she, truthfully, meant very little to me. I let go of her deliberation and instead let myself acknowledge the soreness that peaked every so often as I returned to the cabin and sat down with my back to the wall. Naina pinched my cheek.

"What?" I asked softly as my knuckle rubbed the spot I hoped wouldn't turn red.

"Oh, it's nothing."

She was smiling at me with a purity I had not seen in a long time. It was the same smile my mother gave me when she caught me drifting as I read. She would take the book from my hands and wrap me up in a blanket, coaxing me to sleep.

My bottom lip started trembling at the memory. Tears filled my eyes, so I sat up and looked away, my head hanging low.

"Are you okay?" Amrit pulled on my arm, and Ali moved closer, both worried for something they hadn't seen in a long time. I never cried.

"I want to go home," I whispered. Amrit pulled me in for a hug. I pressed my face into his shoulder, finally letting myself go after holding in for so long, but I stayed quiet. My breathing slowed until it was fairly even, though even when the tears had dried, he didn't let go.

He held onto me until I fell asleep and laid me down in the corner. They didn't speak that night, and I didn't dream. It was peaceful, and for the first time in what seemed like an eternity, I could breathe.

Before the Messenger

CHAPTER TWENTY-FIVE

The Struggle for Freedom

Away from the camps and the horror hidden within them, the winds seemed to blow differently. The East Wind had relayed a message of distress to the rest of the world as his siblings struggled to maintain their natural composure. The North Wind in particular had provoked the people of the nation to act in accordance with the blood of their ancestors. He provided the people with the only fire that could lead to courage and rebellion. Hope.

Hours north of the estate rested the rebellion's most recent victory, Chicago. Their camp hung on the outskirts of the main city, bustling with the sunrise.

"Are the plans ready?"

"Almost," Afia replied, annoyed. Michael had known her long enough to know that she hated interruptions when she was working, especially because she was a practiced procrastinator.

"We have a meeting in—" She threw a knife an inch away from his ear.

"That was close," he breathed. "Your aim has—" Afia turned around and nearly tossed another one when he slipped into the bathroom with a laugh.

Michael's cross hung from his neck as he washed the dark blood off his hands and the dirt that always seemed to make it into his golden hair. He glanced in the dirty mirror and turned back as he saw the face of a friend.

"You made it back alive," he said with a laugh. "I'm impressed."

"I'm not that old," Harman countered with a smile. He turned the corner and changed out of his sweaty training clothes and into his makeshift uniform. "How was the surgery?"

Michael followed him in with a towel over his hair.

"Tiring," he yawned. "The patient coded a few hours in, but he'll be fine."

"You sound like you need a day off." Harman said as he slipped on a jacket before they walked back into the main room.

"We all do. But as you know," he cleared his throat, "the rebellion will not rest until the sun sets on the enemy."

Harman opened his bag and tossed Michael a granola bar before he took one out for himself.

"How are the plans coming along?"

Afia glanced at them, annoyed as her eyes grazed over the words on the page. Her hand clenched into a fist when Harman turned toward the papers, but Michael grabbed him by the arm and pushed him out the door before he could get a chance to look at them.

164

"What are you …"

"I'm saving your life, old man. You can thank me later."

Harman stumbled outside and caught Michael by the arm before he could run off. He pushed him toward their temporary headquarters as people rushed to prepare for their next attack.

"You have one grip," he breathed.

"I have two kids," Harman explained. His hand went absentmindedly to the picture he kept in the breast pocket of his jacket as they walked up the stairs of city hall.

"Dyani called us in for a meeting," Harman said.

"Any reason?"

Michael followed him into the main area and nearly tripped over the dozens of rebels who occupied the space for their own work. Noise filled the large space as they finished the last of their preparations. Their next attack was tomorrow, so they would move tonight.

"She said something about moving up the coup."

"We barely have two months! How are we going to take the south and get to DC before the coronation?"

Harman shrugged.

"Ask Dyani. She's the one in charge."

He opened the door to the briefing room, and they both sat down in their usual seats in the middle. Lena walked in moments later.

"Afia's almost done. She'll be here in a few minutes."

Dyani turned around, and her very presence called for attention as she looked up from the papers in her hands.

"Lena found concrete evidence to prove the rumors." She pushed a stack of papers outlining the information to the middle of the table. "The generals are planning to overthrow the king."

"And they're doing it during the coronation?" Harman asked.

"You guessed it." Afia said as she walked in with copies of the finished plans. She took her place by Dyani and began explaining.

"There are seven generals we need to capture before the coronation. Two have already turned to our side, and one is currently undecided, but the other four have to be taken simultaneously, regardless of if our coup happens during the coronation or not."

"If we take down the generals, we take down the king," Lena added. "He'll be powerless without his district leaders, and we'll be able to walk right into Washington."

Michael leaned forward as he picked up the plans.

"How do we get in and defeat a small army if we're going to split up our forces?" he asked.

"We rally the slaves against them and guarantee their freedom." Harman pointed to the paper in front of him. "It's in the plans."

"Michael's still got a point. We would be stretching ourselves too thin even with the added support," Dyani said.

"We don't have much of a choice," Lena countered. "We have the element of surprise on our side. If we lose that, we might as well lose the war."

Harman looked through the maps and statistics before flipping to the profiles. His hands stopped when he saw the face of a man he used to know as a friend.

"It says here that General Griffin's granddaughter is getting married next month. If we time it properly, we could use it to our advantage."

"You mean plan the attack the day of the wedding?"

"The day before," he corrected. "We would split our forces to take out two generals that night and then capture Head General Griffin the morning of." His eyes were still glued to the pages as Afia spoke next.

"General Jackson would still be in DC, so we would go straight to the capital."

Dyani finished reading through the pages as the others waited for her input. She leaned back into her chair and tossed the papers on the table as her mind shuffled through every possibility.

"Where are Maria and Diego with the restoration?"

"They're almost done, but they need another week before they can move on to the final stages." She stood up, and with her, the rest of the team.

"The Constitution better look like it came right out of Philadelphia with the time they're taking."

Dyani left and the others scattered to fulfill their separate roles, though the coming hours passed similarly, filled with meetings and preparation. The darkness of the night came with anticipation, but it was the only time the people of the rebellion could reminisce, regret, and remember why they had joined the revolution in the first place.

Harman sat up in bed as his thoughts became too incessant to ignore. Moonlight shone through the curtains and fell into the room he shared with Michael. The man could sleep through anything, but Harman couldn't sleep when he started wondering about his family.

He slipped on his boots and threw on a jacket as he walked outside. Rebels guarded the city's exits, but he had made a name for himself in his time here, so they did nothing but salute him as he wandered. He found himself in a park and sat down on an empty bench.

He reached into his pocket and took out the worn photograph of his family that he always kept with him. It was all he could do on a night like this one, hope they were alive and well, wherever they were. He had ended up alone, but he had found himself a family in his comrades. Their friendship had gotten him this far, but he longed for the day he could hold his wife again and laugh with his children. He could only hope that his prayers had been enough to keep them from harm, but there was relief in the knowledge that they were close to victory. He would see them soon, if fate would permit it.

He smiled at the moon, and an overwhelming loneliness consumed him as the wind blew through the leaves. It had heard his message, however, and would go on to carry it to his loved ones.

Wait for me. I'm coming.

Independence Day

CHAPTER TWENTY-SIX

Laughter and Pain

It was silent, and the hum of the bus was the only thing that accompanied the constant beating of my heart. My hands had stopped trembling, but they had taken to twitching when I thought back to the blood pooling out of the bodies. I should have been terrified, but there was something about the scene that seemed unreal. It was too cruel. People were mean and unkind, but they didn't kill as baselessly and mercilessly as the soldiers had. I tried to hold onto the thought, but it slipped away from me as I recognized the truth of my existence.

I had not seen much of the world in my short life, but I had experienced a great deal through books. I lived through fictional characters and learned from their mistakes. The term, humanity, became apparent to me then, but it didn't seem to exist anymore. The very concept that every human, every person had in them an unquestionable humanity didn't seem as certain as I had believed it to be. People were more diverse, I suppose, and for such a deep complex to apply to everyone was unrealistic. I still believed it.

Ms. Garcia had nurtured this hope, and even though it had been challenged by the reality of my situation, it stayed strong. It refused to go and perhaps that was the most frustrating of all, to believe in a world that I had never seen before.

Naina sat beside me with her shoulder against mine, her fear hidden but apparent. I had known her long enough to understand that she was afraid. I had only seen it in her eyes once before at her mother's funeral. She clung to her father, and when he couldn't be there for her, the relatives wanted to say their condolences, she held onto my hand like I was the only stable thing left. Ali tried to make her laugh all day, and when he finally did, it was as if everything had gone back to normal, but it never did.

We found a new normal that day, and another when we started high school. I guess this was just another normal, like everything else, a transition to bring about another part of my life that would lead me to the next.

"Your hands are so cold." She took them between her own and rubbed them warm.

"Put them in your pockets," she said.

"I don't have any."

My words made her cry. It was hidden by the sound of the bus, but loud in my ears. It took me back to the funeral, when we were just kids trying to recognize the permanence of death at a time when we were too young to know that she was never coming back. It didn't make any sense to me then, and I could barely comprehend it now.

"Hey."

Ali slid Amrit's backpack into the walkway, and Naina took it. She opened it at his request and took out the small utility knife he often brought with him when we went camping or to a bad neighborhood. I looked over, confused, and watched as Ali pulled at his hair. He didn't speak, but the action was enough.

Naina ran a hand through her own and nodded. I looked away. I didn't want to watch what I believed to be another reason that proved that this was real.

I wouldn't wake up from this.

The bus stopped an hour later, and the soldiers stood from their seats to announce that we had arrived.

"Out!" We left the bus one by one, the air as stiff as we were, and stood shoulder to shoulder in the snow. A man, the Overseer, walked past us slowly as he studied us like cattle.

"This is the best you could get?"

"Yes, Sir." He sighed.

"They will do."

The men were dismissed with a wave of his hand.

"I will do you this one kindness. Those not capable of hard labor, step forward. You will be set free."

Three men pulled away from the rest.

"Go," he said passively, "before my father makes an appearance."

There was hesitation, but their movements were filled with both relief and fear. They nearly bowed to the man and walked off smiling. I dug my fingers into my palms to keep them from shaking. I could barely feel the wind pressing against my back or the snow melting on my warm skin. I noticed nothing but the crunching of boots on snow and the click of a gun as I waited, silently, for what I knew would come next.

There were three gunshots, each tainting the beautiful white landscape with a crimson as dark as a rose.

I didn't jump this time.

I had grown used to this, whatever it was. Yesterday was another life away, one I felt was slowly growing further and further out of reach, but something had changed.

I was numb. There was too much to feel, so I felt nothing at all. I was angry, but it was pointless. *There is nothing I can do*, I told myself. It was a lie, but it helped me reconcile the part of myself that was still trying to grasp that this was real. I had seen more death in a matter of hours than I had ever imagined. My own seemed nearer as the seconds passed, but even the thought did nothing to deter my mind from the place it had taken. If I died, I would be another body in the pile, another body to burn. My heart wouldn't beat anymore but it wouldn't matter. I would be forgotten.

"Anyone else?" The Overseer casually glanced at those of us who were left.

"I thought not," he said with a laugh. "Take them to my father." He walked away and, with a wave of his hand, sent the men standing on either side of him to push us toward a set of wooden cabins. We filed into the one furthest left, but there was nobody there and nothing aside from a thin blanket and a pair of clothes waiting for each of us. Naina and I changed after everyone left and met Ali and Amrit at the door. The guards lined us up in the front to check that we

172

were all there, and when I returned later that day, all of my things were gone. I never saw them again.

They pushed us into the clean, white estate, and had us wait outside a large, open room. We were sent in, one by one, but I could hear nothing when the man inside talked to them, only the screams that followed.

I stepped through the opening and nearly sighed at the warmth that covered me. I had failed to acknowledge the man in the chair until I heard him stand. Fiery light reflected in his white hair as our eyes met, and it was only then that I recognized the horror of the future that awaited me. I no longer belonged to myself or my family, and there was nothing left of me but my name.

"You certainly are a peculiar one."

I stared into the blazing fire, unresponsive to his words. He swirled the drink in his hands before he shot it back and finished it in one go.

"The weird ones are always quiet," he said with a laugh. The man set down the glass and picked up a poker sitting in the fire. It was glowing, and the circular symbol on the edge was about the size of my thumb.

"What's your name?" I didn't say anything, so he grabbed my face and pulled it up to meet his gaze.

"I don't like to repeat myself, Bonded." The word coaxed the first inkling of emotion out of me since I had left the bus. He smiled and let me go with a push, laughing as I stumbled back.

"Ah, you must be new. Christopher did say that the next batch would be fresh," he mumbled to himself. He cleared his throat and made his voice lower.

"Well, you are an official Bonded under the recent Charter of Veracious." He laughed again. "You are bound to the Charter that was made to protect you in exchange for your voluntary and obligatory servitude, blah, blah, blah." He motioned to the chair by the fire.

"Sit." I didn't. I wouldn't make the mistake of trusting a man so obviously stuck in a world of his own. He sighed.

"If you insist on refusing my hospitality, I will not make the mistake of offering it again. Guards."

They pushed me to my knees and pulled my shirt collar back, so it pushed against my throat. The man crouched down in front of me and patted my cheek like he was looking at a child. He smiled at me, his eyes red in the light of the fire and his skin colored like it was burning. It was the most terrifying thing I had ever seen, a demon in human flesh.

The guards pushed me down by my shoulders until the soft carpet tickled my nose. They kept me down as the man walked behind me, and there was a second of unease before I felt a searing pain near the base of my neck. My face contorted, and my mouth opened, but no sound left my throat. My lungs refused to work until the metal left my skin, so I choked on my own pain. The guards stepped away after a few seconds and left me on the ground as I struggled to push air back into my lungs. My hands were slow as they went to my neck, but the pain soared with every movement.

"I wouldn't do that if I were you." I let my hand fall and pushed myself up. He looked over with a small smirk.

"You are a stubborn one." He said as he approached me, his eyes calculating. "Remember one thing, Bonded. You belong to me. Any disobedience will be met with a pain greater than you can ever imagine," he warned. His smile returned in the second before they took me away. "Don't worry, Christopher will break you soon enough." I was pushed out the back and into the open with the others.

I crouched down and pressed a handful of snow onto the brand. It stung, but numbed quickly like the rest of my skin. I picked up another handful when the door opened behind me and gave it to Naina, and later Amrit and Ali. No one was crying. There was only silent deliberation and acceptance. This was my life now.

There were two men standing apart from the rest, waiting and watching. The first introduced himself as Erasto and the one beside him as Dalmar, his son. They gave us a tour of the place.

"There are three rules," Erasto started. "Do not rest when there is work to be done or they will beat you. Do not speak to them or they will whip you. Do not disrespect them or they will kill you."

As I stood there trembling in the cold, I began to question my value, my worth, and wondered if the condition of my birth was too great to grant me the dignity of humanity. I doubted myself, and for the first time in my life, I wondered if I was truly as disgraceful and atrocious as they believed me to be. There was nothing else that could justify my situation, aside from the possibility that humanity was too cruel for me to comprehend. The latter seemed more likely, but the doubt remained unfaltering in my time at the estate. The truth would reveal itself, but at the time, the thought was the only thing that occupied my mind.

"Stay quiet and obey," Dalmar finished.

His words echoed in my mind for the remaining hours. The work began in the barn before it shifted elsewhere, and the day passed in a blur. It was the first of many, but one I would never forget. We didn't laugh, and we could barely talk. I still remember the first thing I said that night, hours after I had been branded. It was the only thing I had the heart to say. The only thing that made sense.

It's so cold here.

After the Engagement

CHAPTER TWENTY-SEVEN

The Griffin Family

They say youth is as fragile as a cherry blossom. Something as small and insignificant as a warm winter will keep it from blooming, and it's left to wither and fall without a glimpse of the world.

It remains forever trapped within its petals, alone in its self-consuming darkness.

The Griffin Estate remained empty in the years before the war until Andrew Griffin and his wife, Katherine Griffin, reopened its doors. The initial reason behind the estate's closure remains hidden deep within the turns of time, but no more than a few decades had passed before the man returned to his childhood home. A son was born, and they named him Christopher. A sickness would soon rage through the land and in desperation of survival, death would claim Katherine. Silence returned to the estate.

Years would pass before another inhabited the land. She would walk through the doors adorned in white and accompany Christopher as his wife. Elizabeth was their first born, and her very presence coaxed laughter from the otherwise quiet estate. Elijah followed soon after and

Christopher, overjoyed with the birth of a son, forgot his daughter and claimed Elijah as his own. He would take it upon himself to tear away the child's youth and mold him into the man he would later go on to become. Christopher accomplished the first task with ease, but the second was left undone by the birth of his third and final child, Willow. His wife passed in childbirth, and he was left to wallow in his grief.

His son was taken from him, and he was left with only his youngest and most precious daughter, but he had a war to attend to, so he remarried. Regina was tasked with the care of the child, and she grew up isolated between the walls of the estate.

The family remained broken until the promise of wealth filled the cracks between them and returned them to the estate once more.

It was an unusual morning for the Griffins. The sun shone through the windows and despite the accustomed schedule, the day seemed to pass slowly. The dungeon was empty of slaves, and the kitchen, usually bustling in preparation, was still. Only the Griffins resided within the mansion walls that morning.

"Grandfather has requested our presence in the main room," Willow said cheerily as she stepped into her sister's bedroom. There was a blatant lack of color, but Elizabeth didn't plan on staying for much longer than the end of the summer. She would claim her inheritance and return to her apartment in London, soon forgetting the horrors that grasped this nation like a noose. It wasn't her place to speak on a matter that didn't concern her, so she stayed silent as she watched.

"So soon? It's barely noon." Elizabeth stood regardless of her surprise and followed her sister through the door.

Every evening after dinner, the entire family would gather in the main room. There would be little conversation, but they would sit until the clock rang nine before dismissing themselves.

It had become a ritual of sorts. Grandfather wished it, so they complied with the knowledge that their stay was temporary. All but Willow, of course, would leave the estate as nothing more than a distant memory.

The sisters greeted their family before joining the others in their seats.

The general watched the ravaging flames of the fireplace, his thoughts organized and calm. There were five things on his mind that morning, five things that held more importance than the people in front of him. They followed as such.

The stray embers from the fire were burning miniscule holes through his navy-blue suit. He stared at the flames, amused. He had tamed the most destructive element of the four, though it still found ways to slip out of his grasp and revolt. As was the very nature of the thing, he supposed, but it was bothersome.

The next three were intertwined, each representing the calculated advantage of each of his grandchildren. He had made his decision regarding their inheritance months ago, but he often entertained the thought of giving it all away to someone unknown just to watch the chaos that would ensue.

The last thought was lingering and tedious. It was the knowledge that the situation within the border was spreading like a disease. He held no worry with him, however. He had the command of thousands of soldiers at his fingertips. One word, and he could lead even the greatest cities to ruin. It was this very power that stemmed from the root of his problems, but it sustained him, comforted him as though it would protect him from his ultimate end, but Death bowed to no man. It would travel in the shadows and consume his shriveled soul, leaving nothing but an empty body behind. He would leave this world the same as any man, because, unlike humans, Death did not discriminate. It saw people in their truest and barest form, and when it gazed upon them, they were all the same.

The general cleared his throat, and the sound was enough to gather the attention of the rest of the family. They looked up to glance at him, waiting quietly for him to address them.

"The matter of the inheritance has yet to be discussed." He watched their expressions carefully. Willow was bored, as she often was, though Elizabeth had shown interest. Elijah was relieved and Christopher, his dear son, looked thrilled. It was enough to bring about a smile.

"Regina," he spoke with certainty. The air of the room shifted, and he could see turmoil seeping into its inhabitants.

"Bring me a glass of whiskey, will you. I'm parched." The tension dispelled as she left. The general glanced at the clock and sighed. An hour had already passed, though the topic at hand remained untouched.

"Elizabeth," he began. "You may be the first born, but you will get nothing aside from my name. You will forever be a Griffin."

"Grandfather ..." she argued.

"Elijah," he moved on. "You are my only grandson and the successor to the family name.

When the time comes, you will receive the family heirlooms, but nothing more."

"Father ..."

"Willow," he continued. "You are the youngest, barely eighteen, so you will receive nothing." The general shifted in his chair at her disinterest. She had always been an unusual child. "However, after your marriage, Leonardo will inherit the estate and its resources."

Christopher approached the general and spoke up against his father for the first time since his childhood.

"Elijah is my son!"

The general stood, albeit carelessly.

"I am aware," he said coldly.

"He is my heir! How dare you give away what is rightfully his?" The general stepped forward to meet his son's gaze.

"How dare I?" He laughed and his jaw clenched before he spoke next, his voice low and words slow. "How dare I?"

The general backhanded his son.

"How dare you question me!" He grabbed the Overseer by the collar of his white button up and glared at him before his son looked away. Christopher had been defeated, but the general had not yet been satisfied. His anger needed more consolation, more pain, before it could cool, so he pushed his son to his knees and grabbed the poker he had been left in the fire. Its edge glowed like the sun, and in the silence of the afternoon, the Griffin family stood witness to another act of cruelty. They stayed silent, as they had grown accustomed to, because it was the nature they had long since chosen to adopt.

"Elijah, come here." The boy did as he was told, however hesitantly. The general stared into the fire once more. "Hold him down."

He hesitated. "Grandfather—"

"Now!" he ordered. Elijah put his hands on Christopher's shoulder's. The general crouched down and gazed at his son. The sight brought back memories from before the war, when he was but an ignorant and cowardly child. Much had changed since then, but some things remained unchanged through time.

"Apologize."

"I'm sorry, Father," he breathed. "You don't have to do this."

"You brought this on yourself, son."

The general pressed the glowing poker into Christopher's neck, and an ear-piercing scream resonated through the walls of the estate. The man struggled against Elijah's grip, but he stood strong. A small part of him enjoyed this, watching the man who had hurt him writhe in pain. He was a Griffin, after all.

He let go only after the general had stepped away.

"Dismissed."

And with that, all returned to normal. The sisters retired to their rooms, and Elijah found himself on the steps of the estate, thinking. The general returned to his work, and Regina disappeared, but Christopher was left on his knees, alone in the confines of his mind. He would share his pain and release the fury that clawed at his fingertips. One thought occupied his mind.

Blood for blood.

Present Day

CHAPTER TWENTY-EIGHT

A Mistake

It was cold today. The air had taken on a wintery chill that reminded me of the memories I never wanted to relive, but it was easier to work. The fields needed tending, and the mansion had yet to be cleaned. The engagement was done and over with, but I had not seen anyone from the Griffin family since. They hadn't disappeared, as I had hoped, but they stayed to themselves. The change suggested a conflict I took no interest in. I didn't want their lifestyle, with a lavish mansion and dozens of slaves bending at my will. I didn't want power, but only the freedom to make a life of my own.

I smiled at the thought. I wouldn't get a life like that in a nation already brimming with self-righteousness and supposed autonomy. I knew little of our government and its systems, but there was one thing of which I was certain. They were not for the people but instead, for themselves, a government for the powerful.

"Say something."

"Why?" I asked. Ali shrugged.

"It's quiet without Naina, and no one else is here." I glanced at the lonely estate with the hope that she would be back soon.

"Do you want to hear a joke?" he asked.

"A joke?"

He nodded eagerly, but I frowned.

"No."

"Please!"

"No."

"Just this once! I promise."

"Okay," I said, skeptical, "hit me."

"Knock knock." I stayed quiet.

"You have to say who's there."

"Why would I do that? I don't want them to know that I'm home."

"It's how the joke works."

I sighed. "Who's there?"

"Ali," he said.

I narrowed my eyes at him. "I'm not opening the door."

"Oh, come on!" There was a pause, one I didn't realize, before he turned toward me completely. He let his head fall to the side.

"Are you okay? You've been quiet since last night."

I nodded and continued to work. There was nothing I wanted to say, but too much I needed to. I held it in, like always, but it was different this time. My heart weighed heavy with the memories of lost loved ones. I couldn't stop thinking about them, worrying constantly, and hoping, for the love of everything, that they were alive and well. It was too much to believe that they had all made it this far, but I had to. I didn't want to lose them like this.

He didn't push me to speak or ask me to elaborate. He had been through this before, when we had first come here, and he recognized my troubled eyes and stiff movements.

"They'll be okay," he said quietly.

"How do you know?"

"I don't." His voice rang in my ears. "We can hope," he offered.

"We always hope."

"I know, but there's nothing else we can do." He started working again.

"We could run," he said. "We always have that choice."

"We don't have anywhere to go."

"We could fight," he said.

"We're outnumbered and outgunned, and even if we won the battle, there would be dozens more." They would bring in a battalion and shoot us until we couldn't recognize ourselves.

"Then we stay and wait." He glanced at me. "Together," he said. "Whatever we do, we do it together."

I nodded and he gave me a small smile.

"We'll be okay."

He meant well, he always did, but there was something about the phrase that made my jaw tick. The restlessness inside me grew. I was tired of waiting. I wanted to do something. It didn't matter what it was, but I needed to do something meaningful.

It was a selfish thought, and if I followed it, I would break the pact we had made that first night before we arrived here. *Stay together.*

I didn't talk after that. The conversation was enough to occupy my mind for the next hour, and Ali held his silence until it was time.

"That's lunch."

He left to get the others, and I went on, insisting to check on Naina. We didn't always work together, but after what Leonardo did to my brother, I needed to make sure that she was okay. I didn't find her outside, so I decided to go through the back and into the kitchen. She wasn't there either. My hand started twitching as the looming feeling grew in the pit of my stomach, but I continued carefully.

"Let her go!" Naina pushed the man into the wall and helped Imani off the floor. She pushed the girl toward the doors beside me, her orders quick. *Go.* The girl hesitated but left with a small nod that echoed a thank you. In a place where everyone looked out for only themselves, her kindness held more value than it ever would elsewhere.

The man, one I had seen by Leonardo's side, pushed himself up by his hands and ran toward the girl I knew only as my sister. What happened next was a blur.

His knife glinted in the light of the chandelier, and I noticed it a mere second before I reacted. There was no time to think and no real decision to make. I ran forward and stood between them before my left hand twisted the blade out of his palm and my right pushed him back. I didn't wait. I was angry, so incredibly angry. He could have killed her, Naina, the kindest person I knew. He almost had.

I slapped him, my breathing still rough and heavy as he stumbled back into the wall. The sound echoed over the marble and gold, and even the paintings on the wall shook in surprise. I had broken the third rule and now, I would pay with my life.

I was still glaring at the man when the guards grabbed my arms and pushed me to the ground. The Overseer stood with his son. I couldn't see his expression, but I didn't need to. I would be punished.

They took me to the dungeon and threw me into the nearest cell. There were other Bonded in the places beside my own, but I couldn't help feeling incredibly alone as I sat within the confines of the walls that surrounded me.

This is it, I told myself. *I am going to die.*

There was relief in the thought that I would no longer have to face the pain that was at the root of my existence and that no one would curse or beat me simply because they could. I took in a deep breath as I relaxed in the space around me. I never thought that death would be like this. It was quiet, and a part of me was ready to let go, so the pain that often clung to me seemed to disappear. It was not what I was expecting.

My father told me when I was younger that most people thought of the end. It was always on their minds because somewhere, deep inside, they knew that they weren't worthy of the world and its beauty. They knew that they had done nothing but consume and ravage the land, so when they thought of the end, they feared, simply because they knew they were the most deserving of destruction.

To be fair, the notion rarely crossed my mind, and when it did, it never felt real. And even now that it was staring me in the face, I wasn't afraid. All fear had left the day I had been branded to belong to someone other than myself. I felt content, until the one regret I had crossed my mind.

I didn't want to leave them here alone.

The door opened, and the Overseer passed through it in all his glory. A shadowed look crossed over his face as he stopped in front of the metal door. It creaked open, and his eyes never left mine as he entered.

"You attempted to injure a colonel. At the very least, the disrespect is enough to warrant extreme punishment."

I closed my eyes, ready for the end.

"Whip."

That was my second mistake, assuming that he would end my life swiftly as he often did with stray Bonded. When they tried to run or steal, when people were starving, he ordered a public execution. He wanted to scare us, but their deaths never did. I saw them as soldiers dying in the crisis of war or heroes, finally returning to those they had lost. They were nothing less than martyrs.

The guards tried to chain me, but for the first time, I struggled against their grip. I needed to do one thing before the pain returned. It was the very thing I had hoped of doing ever since my first beating. I looked the Overseer in the eye and spat in his face.

That was my third and final mistake. I had a chance of surviving this before. Now, I was doomed to wherever my soul would go after. My faith made that thought endearing. I had somewhere to go where I wouldn't have to worry anymore.

He wiped his face with a handkerchief as I was chained to the cold cement, and the guards exited quietly after they had tied me down so as not to disturb their beloved Overseer.

His breathing was uneven, and it was a small indication of his anger, even though I couldn't see his face.

I will never forget what came next.

The whip went into my back, slicing my skin and cutting through whatever muscle was there. It was quick but not rushed, and the sheer force of the attacks was enough to make my hands tremble. I closed my eyes and prayed for the strength to endure. It was the only way I knew how to get through times like this.

There was a second of relief before the pain returned, and it continued like this for what seemed to be hours before he stopped to catch his breath. It was nothing more than a moment before he tossed aside the whip and brought up his fists. He unchained me and threw me down to the cold, bloodied floor before he began again. He kicked my abdomen until his shoe was gleaming in blood, and when I started to cough it up, he stepped away to shake out his hands. I tried to sit up, but my hands were barely able to push me forward before he kicked me down again. He smiled and stepped on the hand that had slapped the colonel while his other foot pressed down on the wounds that covered my back so I would fall to the floor again. The rough concrete scratched my cheeks, but I barely noticed as the Overseer twisted his foot over my bruising hand. I held in whatever sound threatened to make itself heard.

He let go, and for a second, I thought the worst had passed. I could not have been more mistaken. I moved so that my back was against the wall in my moment of false relief, and he came back with the whip. He stepped on my palm with his leather shoe before I could pull it back, and the pain was enough to steal the breath from my lungs. The Overseer pressed on the limb until he couldn't stand the silence, and when the time came, he lifted his foot and stepped on my wrist instead. The whip in his hand raised before it struck the skin of my palm repeatedly. I counted to five before I could take my hand back, but I didn't look at it. I didn't want to.

The whip returned furiously until everything began to blur, and the pain was nothing short of an afterthought by the time the door was thrown open.

"Father!"

"Let me in," Elizabeth started, "I wish to speak to my father about the inheritance!"

I pushed myself up and leaned against the bars of the wall as the sisters rushed in. Willow looked into the cell before tripping back, and Elizabeth could do nothing but watch in shock when she saw the truth behind the estate's beautiful white walls.

"What did you do?" Elizabeth met the Overseer's eyes with panic.

"Guards," he began.

"No," she countered. Those who had approached moved away. "What is this?" she asked again.

The Overseer sighed. "A punishment."

"That is torture!"

"They get what they deserve, dear. The matter does not concern you."

"Look at what you've done!" she yelled. "It's not justified!"

He laughed in her face as I cradled my bloody hand.

"It's more than justified. It is my right." His voice became louder and more severe with every word. "The vermin deserve no more mercy than the Devil himself. They are more venomous than you can ever know!"

"She's innocent."

Stop, I wanted to say, you're making this worse. If not today, then tomorrow. The Overseer always had his way.

"She?" He looked over. "They all look the same."

"What has she done to you?" Elizabeth yelled.

"Her people have done enough to warrant much more than this."

"She is not her people," she defended.

"They're all the same." He said it like it was as true as the blue sky.

"They don't deserve this." The words brought with them a side of the Overseer only the Bonded knew. He threw the bloodied whip to the ground with enough force to scare the two people who had yet to see his true form.

"They killed my mother!" he yelled. "They murdered her for the twenty dollars she had in her purse, and my brother?

They're the reason he never came back from the war, the reason we couldn't have a funeral because they never found his body!" He glanced at me with familiar disgust as his voice calmed.

"They are the only reason we lost the war. They deserve this."

His talk about family did nothing but remind me of my own. I sent up a small prayer for them with the feeble hope that they were safe.

"Father," Willow moved in front of her sister. "You promised."

The Overseer rubbed his eyes.

"I did," he said. "Are you sure?"

She nodded eagerly with a wide smile.

"Alright, dear."

He dismissed the guards and left with his daughters, one joyous and the other unsure as they left the cold cells and returned to their bright mansion. My head fell back against the wall, and a single thought occupied my mind.

I'm alive.

Present Day

CHAPTER TWENTY-NINE

Lost Ones

The guards pushed me toward the cabin doors, but I didn't walk through them. Instead, I staggered to the showers. It was a ritual of sorts, but it was different this time. The cold water was welcome on my burning skin, and when it stopped, I fell to my knees. I could still feel the blood pooling into my clothes and dripping onto the floor. It was the only sound that accompanied my uneven breathing.

I stood up and stumbled into the wall before I peeled myself off and made my way back to the cabin. I sat on the steps, waiting for the moon to return, and when it did, the wind made an appearance. It nudged me back, but I didn't budge, not until a familiar face shone in the moonlight. I pushed myself to my feet and walked until the pain grew unbearable. Naina's red eyes glazed over when they landed on me, and she stopped as if to make sure that I was really there before she ran through the crowd and hugged me. I held onto her and let out a shaky breath when I buried my face into her shoulder. My fist grasped her shirt and my knees went weak when her hands met my bloody back. She tried to pull away, but I held on, unwilling to let go. I didn't see her eyes widen in horror at the red that covered her hands or feel it when she looked down and pushed aside the slits that had formed in my shirt. I held on until Amrit ripped me away to see how I was.

His hand went to the side of my head and rested there for a moment before he hugged me. The comfort of family was enough to make me forget whatever pain the action would have caused.

"Al-Hamdulillaah," Ali said behind them.

"I need to take her to Miss Lila." She pulled me toward the other cabin.

"I'm coming too." Amrit said. She turned toward Ali.

"Get dinner."

He nodded and ran off.

The women's cabin was similar in appearance but different when one walked through the door. It was cleaner, and the conversation that filled it was not one I was used to. I saw Miss Dae, but she didn't smile like she usually did when she saw me. Instead, she turned away to get the only doctor we were lucky enough to have.

Miss Lila was a kind woman. She had tended to my wounds before, but like so much about today, this time was different. She led me to the back and told me to sit down. It was an alleviating command. Naina sat in front of me, and my head fell to rest on her shoulder while Miss Lila peeled the shirt away from my back. I struggled to stay awake, and it was hard to breathe as the pain pulsed through my wounds. Naina took hold of my hand and squeezed it in what was supposed to be a comforting gesture, but I ripped it away from her, nearly crying out at the sudden pain. I flinched when Miss Lila pressed into a wound and let Naina take my hand again. She looked down at it, and the bruises and blood were enough to make her cry.

One of the other women gave Miss Lila a bottle and a small cloth.

"This will sting."

I groaned into Naina's shoulder as the pain reached its peak and took her hand in my good one. It's almost over, I reminded myself.

"I'm sorry," Naina whispered, "this is all my fault." I didn't hear her, but I knew. We always blamed ourselves.

Miss Lila covered my back with a clean cloth and pulled down the back of my shirt before she cleaned my hand and wrapped it in a bandage.

"Try to get some sleep. It may be hard, but it will help you heal."

"Thank you."

"Of course." She left with a small smile.

I pulled away from Naina and rubbed my tired eyes before I took the piece of bread Ali offered me. I ate with them quietly.

They helped me walk back to the other cabin and sat down by me, the other men too busy in their usual discussion to bother with us. No one made any indication to speak so I did, but my voice was rough and worn in comparison to the others that filled the space.

"I thought I was going to die." They went stiff as I ran a hand down my face. "I really thought I was going to die," I repeated with a laugh.

"Stop." Amrit's voice was strained like my words were choking him. Maybe they were.

"I might not make it out of here."

Naina stared at me, speechless.

"I don't know if any of us even will. I really thought we would, but I don't know anymore."

"You can't think like that," he said.

"I don't even know if my parents are alive." I think I was delirious. I had never spoken like that before.

Amrit grabbed me by the arms and shook me until I snapped out of whatever slump he thought I was in, and when he let go, he pushed my face into his chest. It was his way of comforting me when he knew the pain was too much to handle.

"We'll make it," he said, "and if we don't, at least we'll know that we tried." He pulled away, and Naina cupped my bruised jaw with her gentle hands.

"Just don't give into the fear." For a moment, I saw my mother crouching in front me after I had gotten into a fight at school, her smile kind and assuring enough to make me forget my pain.

"Okay?" she asked. The corners of my lips raised slightly in a smile.

"Okay."

"Get some sleep." Ali said as he turned away and laid down with his back to the both of us. He curled up against the ground in an attempt to hide the tears he couldn't hold in.

"I'm sorry," I said.

"You have nothing to apologize for."

"I'm sorry," I repeated. "I didn't mean to—"

"I know." Ali turned on his back and looked over, his cheeks dry and eyes normal. "I just don't want to think of the worst. It's harder to live that way."

"We have each other," Naina said, "and I know that sometimes, it's not enough."

"It is," I argued, "and it always will be. I love you guys." I punched my brother playfully. "I wouldn't be able to do this without you. It's just, today, when I was in that cell, I didn't think that I was going to come back, and I was okay with that. It doesn't matter if I die, but if it had been any of you instead of me, then life wouldn't be worth living."

"It's always worth it, with or without us. Never forget that," Amrit said. "I've lost one little sister, Meher. I can't lose you too."

Ali sat up, his eyes glued to the wooden floor.

"If even one of us makes it, then they have to live for the others. It doesn't matter. We don't decide who lives or who dies. We just live the life we've been given, and if one of us pulls the short stick, then that's okay." He turned to me with a small smile. "Now, get some rest. Doctor's orders."

It was hard to sleep that night, not because of the pain, but because of the uncertain reality I had found in front of me once more. I had acknowledged the existence of Death long ago, but I had only begun to understand it now. I had witnessed dozens of executions and felt my own life slip away only for it to return again. I had seen pain, felt it myself, and had tended to a land soaked with the blood of the fallen, but there had never been a time when I questioned everything more than now.

I turned around on the rough wood and pushed my face into my elbow as pain shot through my wounds. There was so much I didn't know, and it was suffocating, so I did the only thing I knew would bring me peace. I prayed for the strength to continue.

Before the Beginning

CHAPTER THIRTY

Predestined

I often considered the peculiarity of my birth because it wasn't the beginning of my life, unlike that of everyone around me. My life began much later.

I first stepped into the world as a child, no younger than five, when my father made the mistake of believing that the grocery store would be empty after dark. My mother was busy with her work, and my brother had already fallen asleep, so Papa took me with him. I held onto his hand and jumped around the puddles on the road, still young enough to be confined within the innocence of my youth. He nudged me gently.

"Come on, kiddo." I can still hear his kind voice in my ears, echoing like the sound in a tunnel.

There was only one thing we needed in order to make dinner that night, and it was unnecessary, but still, we walked through the glass doors and into the spice aisle.

I didn't notice it then, but I remember the memory clearly. The argument had begun long before they saw my father. He had no place in it, but it didn't matter. There was nothing he could have done.

I reached for the black pepper in his hand curiously. Papa didn't tell me why we had left the house, only that Mama was busy. *Let's have an adventure*, he said. His words were enough to tame me at the time.

I tried to read the words written on the label, and when I couldn't, the font was too abstract, I opened the lid. My father had walked ahead believing that I was beside him, but I trailed behind, too busy fumbling with the seal on the bottle to notice.

The voices had grown louder and more aggressive when my father reached them. Their anger was enough to catch my attention as I walked down the aisle, and my hand was still pulling on the seal as I stopped to watch the scene.

My father stepped in front of me as a man approached him. He grabbed my father before he could move away and looked him right in the eye.

"What are you doing here, huh? Your kind aren't welcome!" He pushed my father to the floor.

"Your people forced my country to its knees!" The man kicked his abdomen before he could get to his feet.

"Terrors!"

My father stood before the man could hit him again, and with that, the fight began.

A few had stopped to watch, but most, unlike me, had turned away with their heads down. To help my father was to put themselves in danger, and they had families to go home to, children to take care of. There was too much at stake for them to help a stranger.

There is only one thing that comes to mind, now, when I remember the people walking by. The man on the floor was a father, a husband, a brother. He meant more to me than I could ever express, but he didn't mean enough to make them step away from the lives they lived so virtuously. To them, he was just another victim of the time.

The man had bruised my father, and I could see the blood pooling out of his nose. It scared me.

"Papa?"

The man looked over and pulled my father up by his shirt. "Is that one yours?"

I didn't understand his hatred then. I still haven't wrapped my mind around the concept now, but I never had to. I just acknowledged that it existed and that it was usually directed toward me. I learned to live with it because it was a staple of my reality, not because I was ever offered a choice. It was the only life I had ever been given.

I don't know what came over me at that moment. Maybe it was seeing my father, bloody and bruised, still trying to fight off a man double his size or maybe, it was as simple as knowing that someone I loved was hurt and that they needed me. Whatever it was, it prompted me to act violently.

I kicked the man's leg, though it did little, and when he looked down, I threw the spice into his eyes. I had made the same mistake months ago when I insisted on helping with dinner. It burned me, so I knew that it would do the same to him, and I wanted to hurt the man.

My grandparents said that I had taken after my father in this way, but I disagreed. While we shared a similar nature, there was one thing that separated us entirely. My father often felt guilty for hurting someone else, but I never did. I grew up fighting, and there was never time to be empathic when the person in front of me was trying to break my jaw. I didn't want to understand the person on the other side. It made everything more real.

My father pushed the man into a nearby display before he picked me up and ran home with me in his arms. I clung to him, terrified that something would happen if I let go and left him alone. A small part of me believed that I could protect him this way. I never could.

The journey home was short, and when we entered the kitchen, my mother rushed to him. She tried to pull me away, but I refused to let go. *Papa is hurt.* The thought was enough to bring tears to my eyes.

My mother, I didn't understand at the time, was not pulling me away to get to my father. She needed to make sure that I was okay. The very thought of losing another daughter was too painful for my mother to comprehend, so when I finally gave in, her tears, however filled with relief, matched my own. My older brother watched from the corner. He had been out with my parents before, though the instances were less than the fingers I could count on one hand. He may have seen what I experienced that day and recognized it as what it was, or he might have just known that something was wrong. I'm not sure what it was, but the scene made sense to him in a way that it never could for me. He understood the one thing that I could distinguish as nothing more than a feeling at the time, a need to be together.

He walked into the living room and hugged my father. It was a simple gesture, but it was enough to coax a small smile from him. He kissed my brother's forehead and hugged him as my mother held me. Amrit's fear dissipated when he realized that what had happened before hadn't happened again. Papa and I had made it back safely, and that was all that mattered.

I would come to learn more when I started school, where the kids were more hateful and unforgiving. It was an interesting thing, hatred. It festered with age. Kindergarten wasn't nearly as challenging as my first years in the local colored high school. No one called me names or told me that my dastaar was weird. There was no judgment because we were all just little kids looking for someone to call a friend.

Life was simpler then, more beautiful. I didn't have the books I would later come to cherish or the lasting friendship with a hopeful librarian, but there were no bruises littering my skin or bullies waiting by the doors after school. Much changed in the few years that turned me from a child to a young teenager, and things never seemed to look up after a while, but it wasn't something I ever considered. My life had never been easy, but I always had someone to help me fight the battles I couldn't fight alone. There was always somebody in my corner, and that made my otherwise bleak world look as bright as a cloudless summer day. The darkness was hidden in the shadows and away from my life, I believed, but I was naive. I didn't know then what I have come to learn now. It wasn't the world itself that was wretched but the people who had come to rule it. They wrote the laws I had learned to live by and created the boundaries I knew better than to cross. They had taken everything I had ever known because it was too much for them to give. I didn't deserve a family because the color of my skin meant that I was predestined to be a monster. I don't know if that's true. I don't even know if I am what they believe me to be. I just know one thing. My family didn't deserve this.

Present Day

CHAPTER THIRTY-ONE

To Hope Again

It was a new morning. The wounds on my back had scabbed over, and my bruises had disappeared. Everything had gone back to normal, it seemed, but there was a sense of unease that lingered. I was certain that the Overseer would come to finish what he had started, but he hadn't, not yet. I didn't know what to make of it, so I set aside the thought and moved forward.

I was completely alone as I worked on the edge of the property. Erasto had given me the easiest job in the camp to ensure that I would heal properly, the painting of the white picket fence. It was a kind gesture.

"Hello!" I jumped at the sound, and the white paint on my brush splattered over my hands. I turned around and glanced at the girl behind me.

"I'm going dress shopping, and Father says that I can take you with me!"

"I'm working." The fence would take the remainder of the week if not longer. Willow's smile faded and her hands clasped behind her back.

206

"No one else will come." I sighed at her words, dejected. Whether I chose to ponder on the offer or not, I had no real choice in the matter.

"Alright."

"Really? Thank you!" She jumped a little before she calmed down. "Let's go!" She grabbed my good hand and pulled me forward before I took it back. There was a line I didn't want to cross, and this was it, but the action did little to diminish her joy. She looked back at me and smiled before she waved me toward the estate.

I followed her to a slick black car. It was the type of thing I would stay away from as a child. There was only one type of person who owned a car like that, and they were not friendly to people like me.

A man in a tuxedo, one I had seen before, opened the door for her. She stopped in front of him with a wide smile.

"Is Elizabeth coming too?"

Harrison nodded. "Yes, Miss."

She squealed and I nearly jumped again.

The doors to the mansion opened, and two people walked out dressed like they were going to meet the king. Elizabeth faltered at the sight of me, but I hardly noticed her. I was too busy staring at the fields for any sign of my friends. I needed to tell them that I was leaving, but I found no one. They must have gone elsewhere.

Elijah and Elizabeth sat with their sister in the back of the car, and as soon as the doors closed, Harrison opened the trunk for me. I looked between the man and the space before getting in. It was warm inside and dark, very dark. The drive went on for a half hour before I drifted off.

The voices at the front had silenced, and all that was left was the constant sound of the car. I awoke only when the car stopped abruptly, like the driver forgot that he had reached the destination, and it was only seconds later that Williams opened the trunk.

The city was not one I recognized, but, like all cities, it was bustling with people. The buildings shot into the sky, and cars honked until their path was clear, but there was something about the place that seemed entirely new. The people didn't mix in the crowd. They were separated. There were two types of people in this city, those above and those below, the Aryans and their slaves, and we could be picked out by the grey that covered our colored skin and the others by their suits and dresses.

"We're here!" Willow beamed at the bridal boutique and rushed in. Everyone followed, everyone but me, of course. The other Bonded were waiting outside of the shops so I did the same, learning from those who had more experience than myself. My eyes shot around until they landed on a sign in the distance, the words displayed on it interesting but unknown. They meant nothing to me, but it had been so long since I had read something that I couldn't help staring.

Deo Vindice

It was a strange thing, to write a message in a language no one understood. I glanced at the people walking through and from the streets, everyone in their own daze. Maybe they knew of its meaning but kept it from everyone else. I don't know why they would do that, but then again, I didn't understand much of what they did anyway.

I crossed my arms over my chest and stood there with my eyes glued to the sidewalk and my ears open to the passing conversations.

"I will never give that woman another dime!" he said. The people around the man laughed as they followed him to a nearby shop.

"Your thesis on the ethics of Christianity was incredibly insightful."

"Thanks, Dad," the woman said, her smile small but meaningful. I only caught a glimpse of it before I looked away. The person trailing behind them, a young man with skin a few shades darker than my own, was in worse shape than I was. His hands were filled with bags, and his bare feet were lined with scars similar to that on my own, but his eyes were empty and void of anything that would suggest there was life in him.

I smiled at him. He was a stranger, a man I would probably never meet again, but he was human. He saw the world through a similar lens, and even if I would never know him, I knew that I would remember his empty eyes forever.

His gaze stayed on me in the seconds he walked past, and for a moment, I thought I saw a glimmer of emotion.

That was before he turned away and disappeared into the crowd, a mere shadow of the person he used to be. That much was the same for all of us, I suppose.

I don't know how long I spent listening, just that the sun rose and had now begun to fall. I had started to notice a pattern in the people who were here. The businessmen talked about the difficulties of their work, and the students laughed about their previous vacations. The rich complained about the people around them while those who worked for them rushed to get things in order. There was an array of people, but so many of them were the same.

"Hold this, will you. We'll only be a minute."

"Yes, Ma'am."

My breath hitched in my throat as a familiar voice reached my ears. It was too distant to be real, and from another life, another reality, but I searched for it, doubtful and hopeful, and when I found the source of the sound, light tears brimmed in the corner of my eyes. I pushed them back and waited, praying for her to turn around.

Aunt Inaya fixed the bag in her hands and was nearly about to take her place by a few Bonded in front of the shop when she tripped. I stepped forward subconsciously before I moved myself back, patient despite everything. She caught herself and looked up as she stood, and it was at that moment that her eyes fell on me. I watched as she moved away from the crowd and smiled, her tears mirroring my own as they shone in her eyes.

She made a gesture that said, *how are you?*

I gave her a thumbs up. *Great.*

How is everyone else? She wrung her hands as she waited, her eyes filled with worry.

All four of us are okay. Aunt Inaya held in a short laugh at the news, her bright eyes shining. I repeated her question, wondering how my parents were.

It's just me. Her smile grew. *You've grown so much.*

The door to the shop opened, and the woman returned.

I love you, all of you.

That was the last thing she said to me before she walked away. I watched her go until I couldn't see her anymore, but even then, I didn't want to look away. It was like a dream, seeing her again. I almost didn't believe that she was alive.

The door jingled when Harrison walked through it, and it was my cue to act normal, so I let my eyes fall and shoulders slump.

"I cannot believe that just happened," Elizabeth said as they walked outside. Willow smiled up at her sister.

"I am the general's granddaughter. They had to make an exception."

Elijah sighed as he slid his aviators up the bridge of his nose.

"Let's go. I'm starving."

Willow gave her dress to Harrison before she rushed off with her siblings.

"Stay here," was all he said to me. The butler put the bags in the car and mumbled something to the driver before he followed them. I was left to wait again, and it made me wonder what purpose I had here. She insisted I come because she thought no one else willing to go with her. I was her backup, but it wasn't that thought that bothered me. It was being away from my family for so long. They didn't know that I had left, and I didn't want them to think that I had died.

The door to the shop opened again, and a woman walked out with a trash bag in her hands. She looked at the Bonded before passively tossing it to me.

"Throw it away," was the only given command before she slipped back inside. A Bonded seated a few feet away pointed to the alley beside the shop, so I made the short trip there and threw it in the dumpster with the others.

It was quieter here. The noise of the city seemed distant, even though it was only a few feet away, and there was more room to move. I stood in the space for a few seconds before I stepped away, but my feet stopped of their own accord when something in the corner caught my eye. I glanced back before I crouched down and pushed away the littered designs.

It was a bronze coin. I had never seen one before. They went out of circulation just after the war and right before they replaced currency with the electronic system I grew up with. I cleaned the coin with the sleeve of my shirt and looked at it in the light. There was a man on one side and a word written beside him. *Liberty.* I flipped it over curiously and frowned at the words written into the curve. *The United States of America.* It didn't make any sense. There was no United States, only America. One single nation to rule over the people.

I ran my thumb over the smooth metal and folded it into the sleeve of my shirt before I went back to my place by the window display. I stood there for what must have been another hour before the others came back, laughing away, though Harrison looked exhausted as he trailed behind them with more bags in his hands.

Willow stopped in front me and put a small box in my healing hand with a smile. I opened it and stared down at the half-eaten slice of cake before handing it back to her.

"I'm not hungry."

"Really? Okay."

She took her seat in the car by the others, and I returned to my place in the trunk. It was a long drive back, I realized, but the carelessness I could adopt in the darkness had to disappear when the car stopped. Harrison let me out of the trunk and left without a word, so I walked back to the cabins in the cover of night. I was hungry, but the thought was not one that occupied the space in my mind. It was the memory of Aunt Inaya that I played over and over like a recording.

I didn't want to forget it. It was another thing to hope for.

"You need to stay here."

"I can't lose someone else!" I went toward the voice and stopped in front of the women's cabin.

"What happened?" I asked. Erasto's grip on Ali loosened when Amrit turned to me.

"Meher?" His expression went from grief to surprise and eventually, happiness. He hugged me, unable to keep his emotions at bay for any longer. "You're alive," he choked out before the grief took him again. I hugged him back, worried. My brother was not one to cry, and it seemed as though my absence scared him as much as our current situation scared me.

He collected himself and pulled away after a moment.

213

"What happened," I repeated as I turned to Ali. I couldn't see his face in the dark, but the pain lacing his voice told me the severity of the situation.

"She might not make it."

Present Day

CHAPTER THIRTY-TWO

I'm Sorry

I forgot about Aunt Inaya and her smile. I forgot about the coin. Nothing mattered at that moment but Naina. I tried to speak, but my mouth was too dry, and my mind couldn't find the words, so I stopped trying. I needed to see her.

Erasto grabbed my arm and held me back.

"She asked for space. Trust that Lila will do what she can."

I found my voice. "What happened?"

Erasto glanced between us before he excused himself.

"The lieutenant wanted to finish what one of his men had started. I-I didn't see the gun,"

Ali said, his lip quivering as he tried to contain his worry. My hand started twitching.

"It's not your fault."

"I ..."

"No!" I yelled at him for the first time since we were twelve. "God, Ali, none of this is your fault, or mine. We didn't ask for this."

I looked at the cabin, defeated. "Get it together," I said.

Amrit hit him over the head for effect. "We can't be a mess

when we go in." Ali ran a hand through his hair and dried his cheeks, the last fractions of his grief slipping out with his sniffs. We sat down on the cabin steps across from each other and waited. I didn't know how long it was before the door slammed open and Miss Hao stepped outside.

"Inside, all of you. Hurry."

Naina was covered in blood. It stuck to her clothes like honey and pooled out onto the wood around her. I knelt down beside her and forced a smile.

"You look great."

"Of course I do," she breathed out. Her hand grasped onto mine and crimson covered my healing wound.

"Close your eyes, dear. This is going to hurt."

Miss Lila crouched beside me with a blazing knife and counted to three before she pressed it to her abdomen.

Naina screamed.

My eyes squeezed shut at the sound. She was in so much pain, too much pain, but I couldn't help her. I clutched her hand even though it tore at the wounds in my palm.

"Hold on, Bhenji," I whispered. Her body fell limp as her head rolled to the left. Ali turned to Miss Lila with wide eyes.

"I-I-Is she ..." She leaned over and checked for a pulse.

"She just fainted."

"Will she be okay?" Amrit asked. Miss Lila did nothing but offer him a hopeful smile.

"I don't know."

My presence was the only comfort I could offer, so I sat with her that night and prayed for the best. She hadn't woken up yet, and Ali was more worried than I was. His eyes were still filled with guilt, but I didn't touch on the matter. There were some demons we had to fight by ourselves, and this was just one of his.

I leaned back against the wall and took a breath, calmly ignoring the pain that pulsed through my back. There was so much I couldn't control, so many things I had no ability to change, but I never thought much about what I couldn't do when what I could was more important. It was the choice between studying for a grade that wouldn't matter or deciding not to study at all. It was the choice to learn everything I could, even if I had no chance of getting a job. I never wanted to change the world, only to live in it and have something I could call my own. I had found that in my family and now, there was a chance that it would be taken away from me as well.

There was little I desired. As a child, there was only so much my parents could afford, so I stopped asking for things I didn't need. My childhood wasn't filled with toys or expensive vacations, but it was filled with love, and that was enough. They were always enough.

We would eat dinner together every night and go to the park in the mornings. They would take me to the library, and I would do the chores that were never asked of me. Mama was always busy with her work, and Papa was never home until five, but I made the best of it. There were moments I wanted to forget, the mistakes and the arguments, the hours I would spend alone because I was too angry to forgive and too young to understand, but through all of it, I had realized one thing. The people that cleaned my cuts and put ice on my bruises, that made me laugh when I cried and held onto my hand when I was too anxious to do it alone, they were worth more than anything the world could offer.

Most of the others in the cabin were asleep or whispering to each other when I came out of my thoughts. I looked at Naina in the dark and gripped her hand a little tighter.

"I'm here," I said quietly. "Whatever happens, I'm here."

My eyes shut after a few minutes, and sleep took me. I woke up the next morning to the sound of laughter, and for a second, I thought I was back home. My father would open the curtains and laugh at how he knew that I had spent the entire night reading. Maybe it was my mother with a cup of coffee in her hands or my brother, his apple a daily ritual.

I blinked at the light that seeped through the walls and smiled when I saw Ali and Naina grinning at each other. She was okay.

"Ow." Naina put a hand on her abdomen. "You really need to stop making bad jokes." Ali scoffed.

"They're great, and you just laughed," he argued. "Who laughs at a bad joke?"

"I do, when they're that bad." I sat up.

"They've been at it since this morning," Amrit whispered. I shared his smile as I rubbed the sprain in my neck.

"Did he tell you the one about the door?" I asked.

"They're called knock-knock jokes," Ali clarified. She ignored him and turned to me.

"That was a weird one," she whispered.

A man from the other cabin opened the door and waved us forward.

"It's time to go." I stood up with the others.

"Wait for me," Naina said.

"What? No, you need to rest."

"You know as well as I do what'll happen if they catch me in here." She put up her hands. "Now help me up." We did. Wounded or not, there was always work to be done.

"You've got paint duty," I said, "Good luck."

She walked slowly and gave us a thumbs up before we split ways. There was relief in her recovery, but I could see the pain she was still enduring. It was not easy to live.

The hours, filled with the same monotonous tasks, passed by uneventfully until lunch, when I decided to eat with the others by the fence. It was peaceful in the grass, with the estate far away and reality little more than a dream, or a terrible nightmare, depending on which side of the line one lived on.

We ate quietly until I realized that all eyes were on me. I swallowed and wiped my cheek with the side of my hand.

"Do I have something on my face?" They didn't answer, but instead chose to voice the thoughts that had plagued their minds the day before. Amrit elbowed me lightly.

"Where were you yesterday?"

I looked at the grass, ashamed even though it was no fault of mine.

"The Overseer's daughter was going to get her wedding dress. She wanted me to come with her."

219

There was amusement, but it covered the unease that hid in their eyes. Willow's interest in me had crossed too many boundaries, that much I knew, but there was nothing I could do. I had no power to refuse or ignore, even though I did play with the idea at times. I was nothing more than a slave, and she was the daughter of the man I had been ordered to serve.

"Did you have fun?" Naina asked.

I laughed, genuinely.

"That's not the term I would use. I didn't even go inside." I finished the last of my bread. "I did see someone, though."

They took the news absentmindedly, as I would have if it had been me.

I laughed. "Your mother."

Everyone looked up in surprise.

"H-How is she?" Ali asked.

"She's in great shape."

"No bruises?"

I shook my head. "No bruises."

Tears fell out of his eyes at the news, and Amrit hit his back to congratulate him. Naina couldn't stop smiling, but it looked unnatural when accompanied with her pale skin and dark eyes. She flinched when she started to laugh and slumped against the fence minutes later. It hurt her to breathe, and the very thought was enough to fade the bright joy I was currently feeling. I cleared my throat and straightened my rolled sleeves so I could take the coin into my hands.

"I also found this." I flipped it onto the ground and let it shine in the dancing grass. Amrit picked it up and studied it.

"What is it?" he asked.

"A coin, I think."

"Huh." He threw it into the air and watched as Ali caught it. "I've never seen one before.

How old do you think it is?" He gave it to Naina.

"It's not that old, actually. Look …" She pointed to the year on the front of the coin before turning to me.

"Where did you find it?"

"Near a dumpster in an empty alleyway."

A bell rang somewhere near the mansion. It was a clear command, one I hoped never to hear again.

The four of us turned to it immediately, but no one moved. It's meaning was enough to bring back the dread that came with the estate. I nearly forgot I was even here.

"Is it …"

"An execution."

Two Hours Before the Bell

CHAPTER THIRTY-THREE

A Different Tale of Friendship

The light through the windows filled the room as Willow twirled in her wedding dress. Her laughter echoed into the hallway, but there was no one there to hear it, aside from her beloved sister. Elizabeth, out of pure boredom, had decided to join her. There were few words exchanged, but she had become used to her sister, and though she would never admit it, Elizabeth had grown to enjoy her company. Willow ripped the journal from her hands and stepped away before she could retrieve it.

"Give it back."

"I will not," she stated. "You can write in your diary later."

Elizabeth put her pen down with a sigh.

"It's not a diary."

"What is it then?" Willow asked as she opened it and read no more than a few words before it was ripped out of her hands. Elizabeth set it down on the table behind her.

"I'm writing a novel, if you must know."

"That's amazing!" She said as Elizabeth sat back in her chair.

"Father doesn't think so. He says it's a waste of my time."

"He doesn't mean that." Willow's eyes were glued to her reflection in the mirror.

"You would be surprised. Father believes that a woman is incapable of doing anything impactful. He says that my writing will never amount to anything because it is not a woman's nature to maintain the present but instead, create the future." She laughed. It was short and empty of humor, but loud in the otherwise quiet space. "Mother taught me otherwise, but it was always the same thing. Prove your worth to yourself, and others will see it too. She never told me that society had already decided my value." She muttered the last part to herself. It was a small realization, but it made a world of difference to her.

"What was she like?" Willow asked as she looked away from the mirror and turned toward her sister.

"Mother?" Elizabeth said. "She was kind and incredibly intelligent. Her skill with a scalpel was unmatched."

"I want to be like her."

"Well, you've got her cheekbones," she said as she studied her sister, "and maybe even her nose."

Willow shook her head.

"I don't want her beauty. You said that she was kind, so I want her heart."

"I'm sure you'll grow into it," Elizabeth replied with a smile. Yua waited by the door, her eyes clouded with the doubt and fear that often occupied her mind at the sight of Willow. She let out a trembling breath and hid her scarred hands into the sleeves of her dress before she knocked on the open door.

Willow glanced in the Bonded's direction.

"Yes?" she asked.

"Lunch is ready, Miss."

"We'll just be a moment."

Yua bowed before making the short journey back to the kitchen. Rosa was waiting for her near the pantry with a small smile.

"I waited for you."

Yua laughed nervously at her statement.

"Right," she started, "about that—"

"It's fine," Rosa said sarcastically, "because now, you're on dish duty."

Yua's face contorted, but she grabbed her friend before she could walk away.

"No," she stated.

Rosa laughed. "Yes." She stepped away from the others, her limp hidden in the rush, and moved to a more open side of the kitchen. Their chores, for the time, had been completed, so they had a few minutes to talk freely until Mistress Regina finished eating.

"Where's Imani?"

"Right behind you," Rosa pointed. Imani smiled and waved. It was her usual greeting, akin to that of a hello. Yua took her friend by the arm.

"You have to help me."

"I'm not switching duties." Imani signed with her hands and pinched Yua's cheek, "But I'll walk back with you."

Yua sighed.

"How could you side with her?" She shook her friend. "Now I have dreaded dish duty."

"For shame!" They turned to Rosa with wide eyes. "What? I thought we were being dramatic."

Imani raised an eyebrow.

"Yua's always dramatic."

"Well, you're not wrong." Yua hit Rosa's shoulder, but her frown was quickly replaced with a smile. She had forgotten about the pain that came with healing wounds. Miss had not been kind to her mistakes recently, and she paid for each of them, more so than usual.

Rosa rubbed over the bruise on her shoulder, and Imani gazed at her friends, comforted by their happiness. It was enough to see them smile, even if she couldn't bring herself to do the same.

"Bonded!"

Mistress Regina stood by the door to the kitchen, but she did not enter. She wouldn't set foot in a place so readily infested by those below her. It was demeaning.

"In addition to the usual chores, I expect the estate to be spotless by nine o'clock tomorrow." Her eyes darted around the room before they landed on a woman she was well acquainted with. One she once called a friend, but much had changed since then.

"Is that understood?"

"Yes, Mistress." The words rang until the door closed, but the tension that clung to them dispelled with the familiar slam of wood against wood.

Regina's steps were the only sound in the empty hallway, but they grew quiet as they passed by her husband's office. He was in there, she was sure, like always. She did not know of his work, but she believed it was important. He was the general's son, after all.

Regina assumed much but knew little. She never thought to ask about the work that happened on the other side of the mahogany door, and it was not as bureaucratic as she imagined.

On the other side were two things. Novels and coins.

The Overseer was a collector of only the most valuable, and there were just three missing from his coin collection. It was nothing more than a hobby, but it was a dedicated pastime for a man who had little else to do. He kept them safe, and the key never left his waistcoat pocket, but now that the general had decided to prolong his stay until the wedding, his coins had begun to take up dust. They were a secret of his own, akin to the novels lining his left wall. The shelf held a series of banned books, and many of which were unknown to him. He never read them, no, he knew better than to taint his mind with the possibility, however small, that he was on the wrong side of history. He stood with his country unquestionably, but a part of him still wondered, maybe.

The man swiveled his desk chair and leaned back as his eyes glanced over the spines of the novels he swore never to read. *At the very least*, he thought, *they give a little color to this bland room.*

The phone on his desk rang, and he sighed before answering it. He was not a man to be disturbed.

226

"Yes?" he asked.

"The general wants to speak to you."

"I'll be right down, Regina."

He rubbed his eyes and left the cherished solidarity of his office for the reality he had to face. It was tiring, truly.

"You called for me, Father?"

The general was in his usual dark leather chair staring into the fire. It was too hot for such a thing, but it created an aura that devoured him. It was an alluring and incredibly satisfying thing, destruction. He loved it more than those around him could even comprehend.

"Come, sit," the general offered. His hand motioned absentmindedly to a similar chair in front of him. The Overseer did as he was told.

"Tell me, Christopher." He turned to face his son. "How have you handled the Bonded?"

"I did what you requested, beat them, scare them," he replied, casually.

"Do you believe they are afraid?" he asked. "Under your control?"

Christopher shifted in his chair.

"Yes, I do."

The general hummed, and his hand went to his chin for a second before he accepted the drink he had requested. Rosa tried to hold in her fear as she waited for the general to finish.

"Did something happen, Father?"

The general swirled his drink and watched it as its color changed in the fire before he set it down. He was no longer in the mood.

"We have a traitor in our midst."

Rosa nearly tripped over herself as she turned away, but the men were too occupied with themselves to notice the girl in the corner. She bowed before she left for the kitchen where the women were nearly done eating. Rosa opened the door, the sound enough to catch the attention of everyone in the room, and waited until it had closed shut before speaking.

"He knows."

Present Day

CHAPTER THIRTY-FOUR

Death and Hope

The Bonded collected in the space the Overseer had designated for planned executions. It was away from the white pillared mansion and closer to the field and the cabins. The guards gathered and brought us there, to a place where the blood from the last execution was still splattered over the rocks.

Naina leaned into me. It was a gentle attempt to improve an already terrible situation, but nothing could make this better when I knew the person kneeling on the other side of the crowd was innocent. They were always innocent.

Calm footsteps announced the arrival of the man of the hour. His group of guards stayed behind him as he stopped in front of us.

The Overseer was an old-fashioned man. He preferred to execute in a clean, bloodless way that showed both a struggle and the gradual loss of life, so I thought I knew what was going to happen before it did, even if the victim was not who I expected. There was another thing I didn't account for, and that was the presence of the man I had not seen over the duration of his most recent stay.

"The traitor is to be executed under the laws of the Charter." The Overseer's voice was not loud by any means but incredibly collected, poise.

The gravel crunched under his leather shoes as he walked toward the Bonded. His hand wrapped around the sack covering the face of the accused, but he did not uncover it immediately. Instead, he looked at us, and the corner of his lip raised in a small smirk in the moments before the reveal. He reveled in this, the pain, the sorrow. It was the nature he had adopted in return for the humanity that bloomed in the hearts of the rest of us.

He ripped off the sack and stepped away with his eyes curiously watching our reactions.

Amrit grabbed my arm to hold me back, but I couldn't move. I could barely breathe.

"She will be hung for her crimes against the nation." He tilted his head to look at her. "If you beg, I might go easy on you."

Miss Dae looked into the eyes of the Overseer and smiled.

"Go ahead. Kill me."

The words brought with them a tremor. Her resolution was enough to scare a man so addicted to power and dictation that even the world seemed crafted for him.

His relaxed demeanor turned stiff as the command was given.

"She will be hung."

"No." The general said as he approached his son with a small smile. "Give the Bonded a chance. Guards."

They undid her binds at his command, and she stood, unsure but strong. The general walked forward and stood a mere step behind her as he gazed at the field in front of them.

"Run," he said, passively. "If you can make it past the gate, you're free to go."

"Father ..."

"No, son. Let her go." The general stepped away and waited, his eyes calculating and invested despite their bored facade.

Miss Dae looked into the crowd and smiled at the people she would miss. There was no lingering sadness or hesitation when she started walking. I don't know if she knew the truth behind his words then, or if she genuinely trusted a man already choking on the blood of his victims. I don't know what was on her mind that day, or if she was even really present at all, but she was happy. She welcomed death with open arms because she knew the one thing that held true for all of us. Nothing could be worse than this.

A gunshot ripped through the silent air and rang in my ears. Her body fell, lifeless, onto the grass and once again, blood soaked into the soil. The general studied his gun, seemingly satisfied with his kill, before returning it to its holster.

"May this be a lesson to you all. Treachery is not tolerated. Any disobedience will be met with similar consequence."

They left, and with that, released the tension that held tight like a pulled string. Naina grabbed my arm and guided me with the others as we headed back to work, but my eyes never left her still body. I knew she was dead, but a part of me, the same part that refused to cry when there was so much to be grateful for, it didn't believe in death. Come on, it said, get up.

Get up.

But she never did. That part of me stopped trying after a while.

The guards dragged her body away. It would be hung and displayed before it started to decay, and then it would be taken away to be burned like the rest of them. No one would know what happened to her, and after some time, I might forget too. She would be nothing more than a name carved into a piece of wood that would eventually rot away. It would be like she was never here, like she never lived.

"Meher?"

"Huh ..." I looked up, snapping out of my daze. Amrit hugged me in an attempt to provide comfort, but I did nothing but stand there thinking, wondering. Would she be remembered? I pulled away, and the thought lingered for a second before I left to go work with the others.

They didn't talk to me for the rest of the day, and I made no attempt to change the silence. It stayed close with the sun and clung to me after it had fallen. The stars didn't come out that night, and the clouds covered whatever light the moon would have otherwise offered. The wind didn't dance with the leaves, and the animals didn't move. Even the crickets were silent. The world was still and lifeless as I stood there, alone.

It was cold outside.

I pushed open the cabin door and sat down with my family. Dinner was given, and conversation began again.

"How are you?"

It was an innocent question, but one I didn't know how to answer. My hand was still sore, and the lashes on my back were still healing. They hurt, but it was nothing I wasn't already used to. I'm fine, I wanted to say, but there was something keeping me from voicing the words. My hand went to my heart almost subconsciously. There was no sadness, no lingering shock. I didn't feel anything. It was almost as if my heart had stopped beating. I pressed into the cloth. My heart was right here, pulsing rhythmically like it always had, so why did I feel so numb?

A gentle hand touched my arm.

"Are you okay?" Amrit asked.

I closed my eyes and held my head in my hands.

"I don't know," I said softly. I shook my head. "I don't know."

Erasto stood from the crowd and cleared his throat. It was enough to gather the attention he required.

"I'm calling a meeting." Everyone exchanged glances before turning back to their conversations. "Right now," he added. There was shared confusion as everyone moved to sit in a circle. I had only ever been a part of two gatherings in my time here. The first was to discuss jobs and duties the day I arrived, and the second was to address the change in command, but neither had been as rushed as this one.

"A few months ago, I got in touch with a member from the rebellion."

"Rebellion?"

"He didn't tell us."

"We're saved," the people whispered. Erasto raised his voice and spoke through the others.

"They're coming."

"When?" a man in the back asked, and silence reigned again.

"Tomorrow."

Present Day

CHAPTER THIRTY-FIVE

Something to Fight For

Rumors of a rebellion stemmed from long before I was enslaved. The government never acknowledged the existence of such a thing, so they excused it as nothing more than evening gossip that filled the homes of abominations such as myself. It wasn't true. My parents had too much to worry about with the bills and their unsteady jobs, and I was too young to understand the significance of a revolution. I had no preference about who ruled over us at a time when I didn't even know that a government existed.

I had always hated watching the news, but my father would lecture my brother and me on the importance of being knowledgeable about the world we were surrounded by, though the concept always remained unappealing to me. The real world was much bleaker than the ones I could escape to with the turn of a page. But now, with the truth out in front of me, I was nothing short of thankful for the collective hours I spent watching the news with my family. It was the only reason the coming conversation made any sense.

Someone to my right laughed. "The rebellion," he said, incredulous. "That's funny, brother." But Erasto didn't laugh. There was no humor.

"I can assure you that the rebellion is alive and thriving. They've already taken most of the territories, and now, they need our help to take down the general."

"In exchange for our freedom?"

He nodded.

"They need more men." There was a silent agreement between everyone, but Erasto didn't care for it. He had already agreed to something he knew we wouldn't be opposed to.

"Do they know?" I asked. My voice was foreign, more earnest and calmer than it had been in a long time. Many turned to me, surprised.

"The women," I clarified, "do they know?"

Erasto sighed.

"No. They have no place on the battlefield."

"That's not something for you to decide. They should be told, at the very least. They are as much in bondage as we are."

"Kid—"

"I agree," Amrit said beside me.

"Me too," Ali added.

For Erasto, their support was enough to call a vote, something uncommon although not rare. It was an interesting concept, to take everyone's opinion into consideration in place of trusting one to lead objectively.

"All in favor?"

Five hands raised out of dozens. It wasn't even close to a minimum majority.

"Now that it's settled—"

There was a knock on the door. It was short and subtle, but it was enough to bring back the dread that, for a moment, ebbed like an ocean on the shore.

Jasper, the man seated beside Erasto, stood and opened the door. I'm not sure who I expected to see on the other side. The Overseer, maybe, or the guards that patrolled the estate like a prison. It could have been the general, coming to take another one of us to kill. I don't know, but I certainly didn't think I would see the women from the other cabin, standing beside their new leader, Miss Hao.

"Good evening," she said as she walked in. Her eyes glanced over us before they landed on the man at the head.

"There is something that needs addressing. The issue does involve everyone, so I would appreciate if you would make room for the rest of us."

"We are in the middle of a meeting, Hao. I'm sure it can wait."

"It can't."

"Hao ..."

"I don't think you understand, Erasto. I'm not asking."

The four of us were already by the wall, so we waited while everyone else moved to one half of the cabin. The women filed into the other and made a place for themselves.

Naina slumped forward and fell onto Ali's shoulder, fast asleep. He looked over and laughed lightly when she jumped awake.

"Get some rest," he whispered, "we can fill you in later." She hummed and curled up on the floor behind him. Amrit smiled at me as everyone got settled, the action small and hopeful.

"We'll get out of this." His words sparked an emotion somewhere deep in my soul, but it was nothing more than a flicker.

"Yeah, we just might."

Miss Hao started to speak, her voice clear and strong, despite the mournful tinge.

"The rebellion is going to free us in exchange for our help."

Erasto sighed.

"I know."

Miss Hao continued despite the interruption.

"I've talked to the rebels coming tomorrow. The old, sick, and wounded will be taken before the attack begins. The remaining men and women will stay and help with the revolt."

Jasper laughed, and with him, most of the men in the cabin. There were a handful that stayed silent and respectful, but many did not believe her words.

"How will the women help? Will you have lunch ready for us after we've won?" he asked as the laughter died down. Miss Hao smiled at their words, amused.

"The men will help outside, and the women," she said, "will take down the general and his guards from the inside."

There was silence.

"Erasto?" a man asked.

"I don't know anything more than the date and time."

There were no more interruptions after that.

"They will tell us the details tomorrow, but until then, everyone will have to remain as obedient as possible. This is the only chance we have, and we cannot make any mistakes. Understood?"

There were murmurs of agreement all around before she left, her exit quick and subtle. It was almost as if she had never been here. There was a shared joy accompanying the absence of tension within the cabin, but the unexpected weight of tomorrow gave me the ambition that came with the opportunity for change. It brought with it the uncertainty that came with finality.

A part of me didn't believe that it would be over so swiftly, but the other, more prominent part of my heart had begun to let in the anger I had snuffed out for so long. I had grown up fighting, so running wasn't a part of my nature, but I had done nothing but run for the past few years of my life. Survival was such a thing. I had to learn how to walk away and take a beating because I had believed in the simple truth that had dictated my life for so long. I couldn't change anything.

I had watched hundreds bleed and die, their bodies lifeless and cold, and listened to the screams that echoed in the air. It was the very fate of the estate, I suppose, to be nothing more than a cemetery for the wandering souls of the fallen. They wouldn't leave this place with the rest of us.

I would pray for them, later that night, and hope their souls would find peace in the knowledge that we made it.

There was no guarantee that we would, but I would hope, like I always had, that tomorrow would bring the liberation we longed for. I hoped that we would make it out alive and walk out of this together, and that we would leave this prison, hidden in gold and white marble, never to be bound again. I wanted to live for someone more than those above me and spend my days with endless choice and opportunity. I wanted to breathe without a hand ready to suffocate me when I tried to speak.

I wanted to be free again.

Present Day

CHAPTER THIRTY-SIX

Reality and Revolution

I carved her name into the back of the cabin early the next morning. The splinters broke through my skin and scratched the side of my hand, but I didn't stop until I had finished. I stepped off of the rock I had been using as a step stool and took one last look at the names of the fallen, some forgotten, others not yet worn by time. They covered the wall like a mural. It was barren of any paint or color, but instead covered in the blood that colored our history. Each name held with it a story, a testament to the life they had lived and the people they had loved. This was all that was left of them now.

I read every name. *Goodbye.* My hand pressed against the wood. *We're leaving you behind. I'm sorry.* I crouched down and pressed the bronze coin into the grass. I *don't have anything more to give.*

I pulled away and stepped into the open.

"Ready?" Naina asked as I looked up at the sky.

"No, but we should go."

241

We joined the others, and like every other day, the work began. Naina didn't leave to go paint the white picket fence, and Amrit didn't help around as he did sometimes. We stayed together. It was an action that resulted from the words we refused to say. This might be the last time we see each other. We had made it this far, but there was no guarantee that we would live through today, and this was just a feeble attempt to spend what could be our last moments together.

It was an unusual day, despite the apparent normality. The guards kept a strange distance and shuffled in and out of the doors to the mansion. The Overseer had not yet made his daily appearance, and the general, well, he never made much of an appearance at all, but he did today.

It was short and momentary, but like everything else, wholly unusual.

"He's behind you. Careful."

I stepped closer to my brother and glanced behind me as he walked past. It was a man I had not seen in a long time, the supposed heir to this place, Elijah Griffin. He was taking a stroll, it seemed, with a man I assumed was his butler. Elijah was ready in his suit with his hair done in a style that emulated his wealth. He was different than before, too. The previous guilt and turmoil had subsided, and there was a resolve in his eyes that hid every other emotion. He had finally chosen the type of man he was going to become.

"Where is Knight?" Out of everyone in the barn, only one man responded. Erasto stepped forward and bowed faintly.

"He's outside, Master."

242

"Henry, bring him forward, would you." The man checked his watch as the butler hesitated.

"I've never dealt with a horse before, Sir."

Elijah sighed.

"Right." He looked towards us. "Anyone?"

Haru, a man I knew vaguely, left to get the requested horse.

I finished my given task and slipped out to wash the dirt off my hands. I rubbed my palm and flinched as the scabs pulled against my skin.

"Do it properly, Henry. Everyone needs to know how happy I am." He leaned on the fence that separated him from Knight and smiled. The butler took a few photos before returning the phone, and Elijah studied them before handing it back.

"Send them to my editor. I want them uploaded to all of my social media within the hour."

"Yes, Sir."

I watched as he left, my mind wandering back to my previous life as I heard the words that were so familiar. A few kids at school had the money to buy a phone, and some of them even had social media. I was young then, and my youth was akin to that flower that had yet to blossom. I had seen the world but had yet to understand it, and it was in those early years that the majority of restriction was placed on things like books and media. The new regulations never meant much to me. I had only just been introduced to the concept of a written story, and my parents never let me watch anything aside from the news and an occasional movie, but they were a staple of the life I had never lived.

"Bonded!"

There were a handful of guards standing outside the barn with their batons out and ready. It wasn't a new sight, just one I hadn't seen in a long time. The Bonded had only revolted once in my years here, and the guards had us line up just like this. Dozens died that day.

They ordered us forward, and we moved to their will like puppets on a string, but the strings had started to snap, however slowly. We just needed a little more time, but it wouldn't matter if I asked for more, Time always did as it pleased.

The guards had gathered us together mere feet away from the body that was swaying in the wind. Ali grabbed Naina's arm to hold her steady when she, like the noose, began to sway. She rested her head on his shoulder for a second and closed her eyes, her skin sickly pale and cold. I pressed my hand into her cheek, and the action was hidden in the cover of the crowd in front of us.

"You have a fever," I realized.

She pushed herself up.

"I'm just a little cold, that's all."

"Stay in the back and be ready to run when they come," Ali said. "You need to get out of here."

"I'm not leaving you guys."

"You're hurt, Naina. Don't be stupid," he countered.

She smiled. Of all the things she could have done, could have said, she smiled. It chilled me to the core, and for a moment, I thought my heart stopped beating. I forget that it does, sometimes, but at times like this, when unease slips past the cracks in my mind and the worry returns, my ignorance of its presence becomes more prominent. The heart was a fragile thing, often shaken by everything that shouldn't matter, but does. This was just one of those things.

"When you got shot the other day, we didn't know if you would make it through the night. We didn't even know if you were going to make it through the hour, and we wanted to be there," I said, "to make sure that you weren't alone, no matter what happened, but we weren't there in the beginning. We trusted Miss Lila to make sure that you were safe. Trust that we will do the same. Okay? Trust that we'll come back for you." She sighed and nodded, both annoyed and reluctant.

"I'll go." She left to sit behind a tree a few meters away.

The guards straightened as laughter reached our ears. It was the trumpet that announced the general's arrival, and though quietly, his son, but something had changed. They weren't alone today, no, they were greater in number than they had ever been before because today, the entire Griffin family had decided to watch the show.

"We have to be quick, Father. I don't want to be late for the wedding."

The general smiled at Christopher.

"Of course." He turned to us. "Isn't it a wonderful day?" He breathed in the warm air with a smile. "Truly wonderful."

"Father," he urged.

"Patience, son." The smile was gone, and in its place, a calm facade. The chaos in his eyes showed what he had otherwise hidden away. He started walking to and from the corners of the crowd as he watched us.

"Today is the Day of Liberation." He smiled. "Trust me, it's not as daunting as it seems, because today, you will finally be free. Guards!"

The Bonded at the front of the crowd were ripped away from the rest and pushed to their knees in front of the Griffin family. The general wrapped his hand around the gun holstered to his waist and clicked off the safety.

There were five people I knew from the dozen. Five names I would carve into the back of the cabin if I survived. Five smiles I would forget with time.

They struggled against the men who held them down, but the guards were pressing their hard shoes over the Bonded's bare feet. They held the people still as well as they could, but it was pointless to struggle. Their hopes would die with them, and their memories would be left to fade like the color of the leaves between summer and autumn.

The general aimed and fired, and the sound of gunshots rang in my ears once again.

Bang.

Bang.

Bang.

Over and over again until the twelve bodies had fallen. The people, previously full of life, looked empty, and they were taken away only to be replaced by twelve more.

It was at this time that the breeze came and rustled the green leaves and white roses and bloody grass. The clouds covered the sun, but it wouldn't rain today.

Amrit grabbed onto my arm. but I ripped it away.

"I can't watch this," I whispered.

"Then don't look."

My jaw ticked.

"How can you say that?"

He frowned.

"We've been looking away for months, years," he said. "Why is now any different?"

"We have a chance now."

"Wait for that chance. Wait for them. If we fight back now, they'll shoot us all down. We won't be able to help anyone if we're dead too."

"But they ..." *They don't deserve to die.*

"I know," he said softly. "Pray for them. That's all we can do right now."

The general wiped off the blood that had splattered on his white hands, his human hands, before he turned toward the rest of us. He smiled and picked out another twelve to liberate. His index finger, shining with a gold ring, pointed out a random selection. A man by the corner, then a woman near the front, back and forth before it ultimately landed on someone beside me.

Ali hugged both me and my brother before they dragged him away. I tried to pull him back, but Erasto grabbed onto my arm before I could grasp anything more than his sleeve. Amrit held onto me as I watched a boy I knew as my brother walk to his death. They pushed him down with enough aggression to make his knees bleed over the gravel.

"No," I whispered. I blinked away the tears. "No."

He let his head fall forward as he prayed for the last time, and the gunshots began again before he could do much more than turn to us with a smile. His eyes were filled with a light sentiment that spoke to the depth of his character. He was happy that his time had come, and grateful for the years we had spent together. Ali glanced at the sky before his eyes met my own, and I could almost hear what he wanted to say to me, then. *I'm leaving. Don't miss me too much because I'm sure we'll meet again someday.*

A bullet split through the air before his body fell in line with the others. And once again, Death had made an appearance.

A new pain greeted me in the moments after his death, as I watched them drag away his body to make room for the next batch of slaves. It tore at my already bruised heart until it had taken a few pieces. It left me fragmented as I waited for what would come next.

Amrit didn't look at me as I pulled away.

The general picked out the next twelve, and by the time their bodies had fallen, a constant ringing had settled in my ears. I couldn't hear the world around me, and my eyes were stuck on the blood splattered over the ground, so I didn't notice the general point to me until a guard grabbed me by the shoulder and pushed me toward the others.

I fell to my knees as I closed my eyes and prayed. Death had finally come for me.

Three gunshots rang in my left ear before the footsteps moved toward me. I didn't see Haru and Erasto hold my brother back or remember that the blood soaking into my clothes was Ali's. I only saw the general and his bright blue eyes.

His finger rested on the trigger when I stood. I struggled against the guards, but I didn't run. I didn't want to. The gun followed me as I stepped forward to face the man who had killed my brother, and I didn't stop until the tip of his gun rested against my forehead. I had made my peace with Death long ago, and it was finally time.

"Grandfather?" Willow said as she stepped away from the crowd.

"Yes, dear? Ah, right." His hand fell, and the death I had been expecting faded away once again.

I was taken to the girl at the general's command. She smiled at me happily when I came to stand in front of her. It was nauseating.

"Thank you for the gift!" She hugged the man behind me as I stood there, finally realizing the truth.

I was her wedding present.

"I'll take care of her, I promise!"

"I don't care what you do with the thing, as long as it makes you happy."

She took me by the arm and pulled me to the other side of the mansion, away from the eyes of the people and close to a white car.

"What did you do?" I asked, horrified.

She turned around, somewhat confused.

"I did what I wanted to." There was no guilt, no lingering regret. She had no problem with what her family was doing. In fact, she believed in it.

"Take me back. I don't want this." It was a feeble attempt to reach out to whatever humanity I was foolish enough to believe she had.

"I'm saving your life!" she argued.

"I don't want this!" The calm fury had returned as I yelled at her, indifferent to the consequences.

"You belong to me!" she countered, but her facade returned quickly as she calmed again. Her hands clasped together, and she looked away with her eyes glazed over.

"I just wanted a friend."

"Well, you've lost the only one you had," I said. There was no sadness. I didn't care, not anymore. Tears fell from her eyes as she tried to comfort me, but I stepped away before she could. I didn't want her comfort. Her hand recoiled back for a moment before she jumped forward and hugged me. It was an abrupt action, one that initiated an immediate reaction. I pushed her to the floor.

"Don't come near me," I warned, my breathing heavy.

She huffed and covered the short distance between us with a quick step before she grabbed the front of my shirt and raised her hand.

She slapped me.

At that moment, I could see no difference between her and the man I had grown used to seeing in a cell.

"I did this for you," she said angrily.

"You did this for yourself."

Leonardo had turned the corner when I had just pushed her. I didn't see him then, but it wouldn't have changed anything.

He threw me to the ground and checked on his fiancée before approaching me again. His foot collided with my abdomen a few times before I was able to get up on my knees. My breath came out in bloody coughs before he kicked my cheekbone, and my back hit the wall before I fell again. My hands clenched into fists as he picked me up and slammed me against the wall, furious.

"Do not touch her, Bonded," he warned before he let go. Guards bound my hands and shut me into the trunk of the car. I turned to my side and covered my head with my arms as the sound of gunshots filled my ears. I blamed myself for this. I had been the one who had foolishly mistaken her decency for kindness.

"You're going to love my wedding dress." She laughed.

I didn't say goodbye.

"I'm sure I will."

"Do you think Father will be late to the wedding?"

"It shouldn't take more than a few minutes," he said.

I closed my eyes as my mind struggled to keep the grief at bay, but somewhere in the chaos of my mind, a memory resurfaced, one I had nearly forgotten.

Before the Beginning

CHAPTER THIRTY-SEVEN

A Winter Memory

It was years ago in a time I didn't remember as anything other than perfect. I was a child, young and naive, but too innocent to care. The snow had fallen well the night before, and my brother's elementary school had cancelled all of his classes. It was the first snow day that I ever remember. The four of us, bundled up in coats and old shoes, walked the short way to the park with Aunt Inaya and my mother.

"We should build a snowman!" Naina said as she jumped up and down in the snow covering our path. Ali shook his head.

I want to make snow angels. I couldn't hear his voice in my ears. I remembered his young smile and his bright eyes, but I couldn't remember the sound of his voice.

I slipped on a hidden sheet of ice and fell forward.

Pain was different to me then, still unknown and foreign. I grew out of my clumsiness as I got older, but at the time, I knew it as nothing more than another part of my simple life.

The cold snow dug into my hands as I pushed myself up, and my bottom lip began to tremble as tears filled my eyes. My brother helped me up and brushed off the snow that stuck to my clothes with a smile.

"Don't cry," he said.

He offered me a hand, and I took it, the momentary pain forgotten.

We all ran toward the playground as soon as we could see the swings, and my mother, laughing at our excitement, sat down on a bench with Aunt Inaya. The wind was gentle that morning, and even though the cold was spirited, it was not bitter.

I played with them until my cheeks turned pink and my hands got dry. I don't what led me to do what I did next. I was never a spontaneous child, but my curiosity had gotten the best of me as I wandered toward the trees to follow the noise that led me away from the safety of the playground. I walked a little further and found an Aryan girl crying behind the cover of a tree.

"Hello."

She sniffed and wiped away her tears.

"Hi," she replied.

"Do you want to play with me?" I asked.

She hesitated.

"I want to go down the slide," I said. She smiled and looked over at the playground.

"Me too!" She stood up and ran back with me, joining in with the others like she had known us for years.

I was so happy to have another friend that I forgot to tell my mother. The girl's parents were nowhere in sight, and I knew that Mama would be upset that I was playing with a stranger, but the thought never came to mind.

"Hey!" An older boy, maybe twelve or so, jogged toward us. We were in the middle of building our snowman, Mr. Snow. He was a mess, I remember, but so beautiful.

"Get away from her, Terrors."

I didn't know why he was so angry. We were just kids, but it didn't matter, I guess. We were born monsters.

He pushed the first person he saw, Ali, who fell back into the snow. The boy pulled his sister behind him roughly before coming at my brother, but I, being the protective child I was, did the only thing that came to mind. I threw a snowball at him.

It hit his face, and the surprise was enough to make him stumble. He was like a bull, that boy, when he recovered from the impact. He charged right at me, and his fist, covered in a few rings, connected with my cheekbone.

The fight had begun.

He was taller and older and stronger, but it was four to one. We didn't win by any means, but the noise of four struggling kids was enough to catch the attention of Aunt Inaya who ran towards us faster than I had seen her ever run. She yelled at the boy, and it was enough to scare him away.

I still remember his sister, the sweet girl with the deepest emerald eyes I had ever seen, waving as she followed him. I'm not sure if she remembered me. I never saw her again, not at the playground or in the neighborhood. I don't know what happened to her, if she grew up to be like them, or if she held onto her heart.

I was crying when my mother saw me, so she took us home. My father was in the office, reading. He could do that when I was young, call in sick, but he had never missed a day these past few years. He didn't want to lose his job.

My father made my brother and me hot chocolate while my mother cleaned the blood dripping from the cut under my eye and iced my brother's bruises.

"Mama?" I asked.

She hummed.

"Did I do something wrong?"

"No, dear," she said softly.

"Then why was that boy so mean?"

She shared a glance with my father.

"Who wants hot chocolate?" he asked with a smile. I raised my hand high.

"I do!"

"Careful," he said, "it's still a little hot." So, I waited and blew on it without a care in the world. I had forgotten about the throbbing pain and the fight as the boy and girl became somewhat of a distant memory.

My father crouched down with a smile.

"Your mother tells me that you two were real warriors."

I smiled back at him.

"Like the ones in the stories?" I asked. The same stories I grew up to know as my history, filled with fearless warriors and saints and the martyrs I remembered and looked up to because they were fiercely loyal. I didn't grow up with superheroes or princesses. I never even thought they were made for me. They didn't share my skin or my dastaar or even my language so, as a child, I never believed that I could be anything like them.

"Yeah," he said, "just like in the stories." A thought popped into my mind.

"Is there anymore?"

"Finish this first, and then you can have more," my mother said. I slipped off the couch and gave my still cooling drink to my mother.

"I want to share. Can I share?" They laughed and left to get their coats.

It was a funny time to relive a memory like this now, still stuck between those four walls, but there was no remorse with this memory. I guess it was still too young and untainted, still a child's memory. I could understand more of the world now, but the lingering happiness was still there accompanied with an unusual sense of pride. It was the memory of my first fight. Many more would come with time, and the pain that followed gradually grew with age, but there was something special about the way I remembered it. The fight itself wasn't the climax. It wasn't the most important thing; no, that came a little later with my father.

We're like the warriors in the stories, I remember thinking.

I turned in the darkness of the car as I calmed down, finally remembering who I used to be and who I still was, deep down. I was a fighter, a warrior, and much more than what I had been forced to become.

I took in a quick breath as my decision became final. I was leaving, one way or another, and getting back to my family. I had made a promise, and it was one I didn't plan on breaking anytime soon. Stay together.

Present Day

CHAPTER THIRTY-EIGHT

A Chance for Freedom

I kicked the back of the trunk over and over again as my neck strained in the confined space and my cuffed hands grew excessively numb. My bare feet pounded against what felt like a wall. I would never be able to break through it, but the sound was enough to catch their attention. The car stopped, but I didn't stop kicking until a door slammed closed. The sound was muffled, though not much louder than the sound of my heart pounding in my ears as I waited. I stopped almost mechanically and moved so that I was crouched right in front of the opening.

The trunk unlocked, and the walls suffocating me shattered like glass. I pushed against the back of the trunk with my feet and propelled myself forward. My shoulder collided with Leonardo's rib cage as I flew into the air. It was a split second, but it meant everything. My body fell onto the road, and the pebbles littering the asphalt dug into my skin and branded me with new cuts and scrapes. I blinked past the blinding light of the sun and pushed myself to my knees, my head falling forward in the moment I took to breathe. Willow stepped out of the car and gasped as I turned, her eyes focused on the man still on the ground. Pain was new to him. It was no longer exotic or peculiar, instead excruciating, and torturous.

I pushed myself up to my feet and looked down on him, my breathing heavy. I wasn't nearly as angry at him as I was angry at her, but it didn't matter. They didn't matter. I had to get back to the people who did.

My shadow fell over his gasping form as I watched him. It was an interesting thing, to see a man so incredibly self-righteous be trembling in the middle of an empty road. It should have been thrilling and exceptionally glorious, but it was nothing like that. When I looked into his fearful eyes, I felt nothing but pity.

A click caught my attention.

"Get away from him!" Willow raised the gun and aimed it at my heart with both hands. I did nothing but stand there, watching her. I couldn't understand why she feared for him, a man so obviously caught up in a world of his own.

A bullet split through the air.

I stumbled at the sound of a gunshot and nearly fell to my knees as a searing pain pulsed through my shoulder. I didn't actually think that she would do it, but she shot me.

She shot me.

I pressed my hand to the wound and looked at the blood glistening on my skin. This was different. It was no longer just a wound, either purposeful and torturous or simply accidental. This was a battle wound. It was remarkable to feel a pain that meant so much more than what I had grown used to. It marked me as the warrior my father had believed me to be. It redeemed me.

Willow's eyes were squeezed shut, and her hands shook furiously as the sound echoed. I stepped forward when Leonardo tried to move away and pressed my foot against his throat before he could get up. She opened her eyes, and the gun fell from her hands.

"No! Let him go," she ordered, but I pushed down further.

"The keys," I said. "Now."

That strange voice had returned in place of mine. I had heard it once before on the day in the coffee shop, the same day I was taken. It was calm and low and angry. It must have scared her because she did what I said without question. The keys rattled as she rushed over to me, the gun growing cold on the road a few feet away, and the sound didn't leave my ears until my wrists had been freed of their cuffs.

"The gun," I said, though she hesitated. "I will not ask again."

Leonardo choked and grabbed at my ankle as he struggled for air, but he did nothing more. She watched him for a second, her face pale, before she picked up the gun. Her gaze lingered on the metal as she turned around.

"If you shoot me, he'll be dead before I fall," I warned. She glanced at me, thinking. I was stiff as I waited and ready to move away just in case she decided to do again what she had done before, but she didn't take the chance.

The gun felt cold in my hand.

I took one last look at the man on the ground before stepping away. Willow ran to him with a terrified sob. I still didn't understand her fondness of him. I never would.

I checked the bullets in the magazine and got a rough estimate before sliding it back. I had shot a gun before, though it was not a memory I liked to remember, but it felt familiar in my hand. Leonardo stumbled to his feet, and when he did, I aimed it at him. He grabbed Willow by the arm and attempted to push her in front of him, but she slipped out of his grip and moved closer to the car.

"You helped kill my brother." I stepped forward. "Shot my sister." Another step. "And murdered dozens." He was standing at the edge of the road with nowhere else to go, trembling in fear.

The wind ruffled my worn clothes as it flew past the world, watching but doing nothing more. It was comforting.

"You don't deserve to live."

The sound of shoes slipping against the asphalt reached my ears before I could move. It was coming from the direction of the estate, from the very prison I had only just escaped from.

Elijah stopped when he saw me, and Elizabeth nearly ran into him. Their breathing was heavy and uneven, and their demeanors shaken. They were afraid, I realized. They were all so afraid.

There was a crazed look in their eyes as they waited for what I would do next. I could shoot them. I could, because they were one of them, Aryan. They were the children of the man that had tortured and murdered hundreds. Their grandfather had initiated this genocide. He was responsible for this, all of this, but even aside from their lineage, they were not good people. A part of me wanted to end this, not for myself, but for the fallen, for Ali and Miss Dae and all of the others who had died too soon, but as I looked at them and gazed into their eyes, I saw the little girl with a bright smile. I saw Noah, a compassionate boy who shared their likeness but not their heart. I saw the life that glowed in all of us.

I pulled the trigger.

Leonardo screamed as he fell, his hand clutching his wounded shoulder like the sky had fallen. Maybe it had. I shot him again, wounding the very leg that had kicked my brother.

"You monster!" Willow yelled. I ignored her with the knowledge that Leonardo would live. His wounds were scratches compared to my own.

My hand fell to the side, the gun still warm and smoking.

"Go," I said quietly to the rest of them.

They rushed into the car and drove off without another thought. I could hear the tires slipping against the asphalt as I ran back. My bare feet were stamped with a crimson color, but I didn't feel any pain, and I didn't turn back to see my bloody footprints against the black road. I only looked forward.

Present Day

CHAPTER THIRTY-NINE

Chaos and War

I ran past the gates of the estate, and the sound of gunshots rang in my ears as I got closer and closer to the battle. I dodged rogue bullets and tripped over limp bodies as grenades ripped through the mansion. People ran at each other from both sides with solely their fists, but nothing separated one from the other aside from the clothes on their backs.

The rage and fear in their eyes was so familiar. I had seen it hundreds of times before, and I was sure that I would see it a hundred more, but the feeling they brought with them was always the same. A cold eeriness.

Two men fought in front of me. One had darker skin than the other, but still, they looked like brothers. He swung around a knife while the other dodged, the actions abrupt and uncalculated, for as quickly as everything happened, it was over in a matter of seconds. The man on the left stumbled on a rock, and the other took advantage of the opportunity. He grabbed the other by his shirt and pushed the blade into his heart. Their eyes met and there, for no more than a moment, I thought I saw a glimmer of remorse, of pain. The body fell,

262

and he moved on to kill another, and another until eventually, his body joined the others resting on the grass.

I moved on quickly, and no one really noticed me. That was the plan, to slip past and find the others before it was too late.

A man attacked me suddenly. I barely dodged his fist in time, and my feet stumbled over themselves in an attempt to stay alive. His hands wrapped around my throat and pushed me into a rough surface. His eyes were filled with raging fury as I moved against him to loosen his grip. I struggled to pry away his hands and breathe. I just wanted to breathe.

The gun had fallen out of my hand and landed somewhere in the dirt, so I was left on my own. I pulled my legs up and kicked him as hard as I could. He fell by the corpses and struggled, as Leonardo had, to catch the breath that had been so forcefully taken from him. It was a familiar feeling. I was practically gasping as I picked up the gun and aimed it at him, my hand steady and my finger stiff despite my trembling soul.

It was so easy to kill. With one shot, he would be dead. His body would mix with the others, and he would be nothing more than another sacrifice, another life taken in the name of the general. It was the decision of a second, but it held with it the weight of the world. I had been fighting my entire life, and I knew that I would have to fight for the rest of it, but I didn't want to kill. He was a son, a brother, maybe, or a father and though, at that moment, I had put little value on his life, I knew that someone was waiting for him to come home, just as my father had waited for his brother, and I had waited for my sister, someone was waiting for him too.

I pulled the trigger.

He cried out as he grabbed his bleeding leg, and I moved on.

The screams of the wounded blended with the gunshots until I realized that I could hear nothing aside from the constant beating of my heart in my ears. It was deafening.

A bullet grazed past me, and I took it as a warning to hide and wait. I crouched behind the remnants of a shed and searched for my family, my stomach uneasy. The scene in front of me was a blur of movement and noise and blood, so much blood. I stood, hoping to get a better view, when I stumbled into the wall beside me. Pain cracked through my mind, but I blinked past it and returned again to my place near the edge. I took a single step forward, nothing more, but it was enough to make me stumble again. My vision blurred as the headache returned.

There was movement close to me. I turned around and nearly shot the Aryan man as he stood with his hands up in a motion of surrender. He was in rebel clothing, and the patch on his arm was the only variation.

"I'm a medic," he said. My jaw ticked as my inner turmoil returned. I had to remind myself, as I often would in the future, of the one truth that defined us all.

They may share the same skin and the same eyes, but it does not mean they will share the same heart.

I put the weapon away and sat down. He knelt next to me and inspected the wound before stopping the bleeding. There were no words exchanged, no sentiments. The golden cross around his neck glinted in whatever shine was left of the sun as I waited for him to finish.

"Michael?" A woman in a similar uniform crouched down by him, though her attention was still on the battle.

"Almost done, Lena." He glanced at me. "This will hurt." I barely flinched as he pressed disinfectant into the open wound and wrapped it.

"They've almost got him," she said.

"Any orders?"

"Hold off enemy soldiers." He wiped the blood from his hands and stood up with his gun.

"Can you walk?" he asked. I nodded. "Then we have to go."

"I need to find my friends," I said. His gaze lingered on me for a moment as a thought passed his mind.

"They're probably with the others by the cabin."

I got to my feet and turned towards the battle before I ran to the place I had left Naina. The man tried to call me back in a feeble attempt to keep me away from the chaos of war, but I disregarded his words as I ran through the heat of the battle. It was fifteen seconds of foolishness, fifteen seconds that could have gotten me killed, but it was in those fifteen seconds that I realized that the future was as predetermined as the past, and that life was too momentary for worry.

I slid to my knees as I turned to the back of the tree. Naina moved her head slowly when she noticed movement, and she met my gaze with a smile. Her face had grown even paler, and the light in her eyes had begun to fade. I didn't want to believe it; I couldn't believe it, so I ignored the signs.

"Naina, I'm here. Look at me." I touched her arms when she closed her eyes. "I-I came back for you."

Her eyes fluttered open, and her smile returned, but I could see the exhaustion that weighed heavy in every movement. She was ready to go, but I wasn't ready to let go. I couldn't lose someone else, not when we were so close to the freedom we had been dreaming of for so long.

"Naina, please," I pleaded.

She took my hand in hers, and I leaned forward as she spoke.

"You're bleeding," she whispered.

"I shot Leonardo," I told her. "I got him back for hurting all of you." She pinched my cheeks before turning away to cough.

The Aryan medic from before rushed behind the cover of the tree in an attempt to keep himself protected from the nearby battle. He glanced at the new wound on my arm caused by a rogue bullet, but it was before he noticed the girl against the tree. His eyes glanced over her once before he moved to kneel beside her. There was no obvious source of injury, so he did the next best thing.

"Where does it hurt?"

"Everywhere," she breathed out.

"The bullet wound," I remembered. "She was shot a few days ago."

"Right," she said as she laughed lightly and lifted up the corner of her shirt to reveal the bandages. When the medic undid them, it showed what had been previosly hidden. Dark bruising just around the wound covered the left side of her abdomen.

"Hematoma," he whispered. She coughed again, though fear accompanied the sound this time. He glanced at me with an apologetic expression.

"No," I turned to her. "H-Hold on. We—"

"It hurts. It really hurts." Her voice trembled as she gripped my hand. "I don't want to be alone. Don't go."

"I'm right here." I pushed back my tears as I struggled to calm my breathing.

"Stay," I pleaded.

"I can't." She shook her head as her vision blurred. "I don't want to suffer anymore. I can't handle the pain."

"Naina …"

"Please," she begged, and I forgot my own pain to carry hers.

"Okay," I whispered. I didn't look at her, and I couldn't come to terms with another loss, so I did the only thing that would bring her comfort in that situation. I moved forward and held her in my arms for the last time. It was the reassurance that came with family, and the promise that I loved her for all of her scars. She would leave this world knowing she wasn't alone, and that was the most powerful thing of all.

The void in my heart had grown, and when I walked away a few minutes later, more pieces had fallen away, leaving me emptier than before.

The medic ushered me forward, and I followed closely behind as he moved from place to place. The dizziness returned every so often, but I pushed past it. Now was not the time. My breathing grew unusually heavy as I stumbled again, but I ignored it. I had to get to my brother. I had to keep my promise. He was all I had left, and I couldn't lose him now, not when I had already lost them both.

I followed the medic past the corner of the estate and toward the side with the cabins. A group of people, the old and wounded, were under the protection of a handful of soldiers. I went toward them.

I had made it into the crowd when a hand pushed me. I frowned and glared at the person before I realized who it was.

"Veere." He hugged me, and I returned the gesture with one of my own. I pulled away, but I couldn't bring myself to smile.

"You gave me a scare," Amrit said. He was walking with a slight limp, and there was fresh blood over his bandaged leg.

"She's gone," I said.

"What?"

"Naina didn't make it." It took him no longer than a minute to acknowledge her death and compose himself.

"You're so cold," he said.

"I'm fine."

"You're—"

"Meher?"

Never in my life had I hoped for anything more to be real than in that second. I didn't turn toward the voice. I couldn't. I didn't want to find out that it wasn't real. Amrit rushed toward the man behind me as I stood there, stiff. I closed my eyes and took in a deep breath. I had to know.

I turned around and nearly fell to my knees. There, in the light of the sun, fitted into a rebel's uniform, stood my father.

"Papa?"

I didn't think he was real. He couldn't be.

He smiled as I approached him, and his hand came to rest on the side of my head like it used to a lifetime ago. I hugged him and cried quietly into his chest. For the first time in years, I didn't keep it in. He held onto me like he was afraid, like that day at the supermarket when I was a child.

He pulled away to see how much I had changed.

"How are you?"

"Great," I said with a bright smile, my thoughts still scrambled. "The color suits you,"

He laughed through the tears in his eyes.

"Thanks."

His hand came to rest gently on my cheek.

"You look so much like your mother, and you," he put his hand on my brother's shoulder, "have gotten so tall."

Amrit laughed. He hugged us again and joy overflowed in our small corner of the world.

"Where's Mama?"

The light in his eyes dimmed as he pulled away.

"I don't know," he said. "I haven't seen anyone since they took you away." He frowned as he noticed my shoulder.

"You're bleeding."

"It's nothing," I said. "I'll be fine."

I don't know if he believed me then. I don't think he did, but circumstances were such that there was nothing he could do. He remembered something.

"Are you hungry?" he asked. I grinned as he reached into his pocket and took out a chocolate bar.

"Share," he said, before he gave it to my brother.

"Harman!" Someone shouted his name somewhere to my left.

"That's my cue. You kids stay put, and don't get into too much trouble." He hugged my brother and kissed my forehead before he left with the others. I watched him go, and in the very depths of my soul, some of the light had returned.

After the War

CHAPTER FORTY

Finally, Free

I was surrounded by death.

The gunshots, previously bountiful and thunderous, had silenced, and the people had stilled, either standing to watch the victory they had worked for or lying lifeless in the mix of enemies and friends. Bodies covered the ground like a blanket, and the blood that had sprayed over the white roses and dropped into the soil was nothing but a testament to the fate of this world.

The mansion, now ruined with dirt and ash, was in pieces, and from the rubble emerged three, the general, the Overseer, and his wife. They shared the fate of their broken mansion and were now left on their knees with nothing but a scorched legacy and a memory of the power that was once at their fingertips. They hadn't believed that it would lead to this, but even if they had known, there was little chance they would mend their mistakes. Power was such a thing.

"This is it, huh?" Amrit breathed out. "I'm not going to miss this place," he said as he wrapped an arm around my shoulder.

"We made it," he said.

"They didn't."

271

"America will burn without me," yelled the general. "I made this country! Me!"

"Oh, shut up," said the woman tasked with containing him.

"How dare ..." She pushed his head into the dirt with her foot.

"I don't like to repeat myself. Understood?" When he didn't answer, she dug in further until he could barely see.

"Yes," he choked out. She let go, and a small smirk graced her face as she turned away.

A thought crossed my mind.

"Do you know where Papa is?"

He shook his head.

"I'm sure he's around here somewhere. Why?"

"I need to do something." I left Amrit to look for my father, and when I found him standing with a group of rebels, I assumed that he was busy, so I searched for someone else who could help me. There were a few soldiers wandering freely, but only one I recognized.

He was standing by the others, but he didn't converse with them. He just stood there.

"Does it hurt?" he asked as I approached him with his eyes on the wound. "I don't have much to help with the pain." I hesitated as he checked around his pack for a painkiller.

"Do you have some paper, and a pen, maybe?"

He stopped and reached into his breast pocket to take out a journal and a small pen.

"Will this work?" He offered it, and I took it into my hands. It had been so long since I held something so similar to a book. I nodded.

"Thank you."

I started walking toward the cabins, and the chatter faded behind me as I reached the back. The names were silent against the wood as I wrote them down, one by one, in addition to the names of my friends and the other Bonded that had fallen today.

The ink sunk into the worn paper as I marked it, and the pen felt natural in my hand, even though I had not held one for so long. The seconds grew into minutes before my hand began to strain. I shook it out before I finished writing the few names that were left.

The medic returned.

"Your father is ... Oh my God," he said as his eyes raked over the back of the cabin. I ripped out the sheets of paper and returned the borrowed items. He took them absently but did not otherwise move.

"They're gone," I said.

"There are so many."

"These are only the people that have passed in my time here. There are more." He gazed at them for a moment longer before he turned away.

"Your father's looking for you."

It was odd to walk side by side with a man that, only yesterday, I wouldn't have trusted. He had been kind, though, and I suppose that was enough.

We went past the cabins and neared the estate where the others had settled. Right by the soldiers were a group of people, the enemy, waiting on their knees to be taken. I almost looked past them, almost made the mistake of ignoring the small motion that everyone else had missed.

The general jerked his shoulder upwards. It was an unusual movement, but one I recognized. I had been bound enough times to understand what the soldier guarding him did not.

He had freed himself of his binds.

General Griffin tackled the rebel and grabbed his gun. He aimed it at a group of people in front of me and was about to pull the trigger when another rebel pushed him down. His arm remained steady as he elbowed the rebel and aimed. I looked in the direction of the gun.

"Look out!"

I ran towards my brother, but it was too late. I was too far away. He turned toward me, confused. Papa glanced at me before he looked forward and saw what Amrit had not. He pushed him out of the way as the deafening sound of a gunshot rang in my ears once more. My brother fell into the dirt as Papa stumbled, blood soaking into the cloth covering his abdomen. My feet stopped. I couldn't move. I couldn't think. I could barely breathe.

No, no, no, no, no.

I watched as he pressed his hand to the wound. I watched as he fell. I watched, terrified, as people rushed to help him. The medic ran past me, and as his shoulder knocked into mine when he reached for his equipment, I remembered how to move again. I ran to my father and fell to my knees beside him.

"Papa?" His bloody hand caressed my cheek.

"My beautiful little girl." Amrit crouched down beside me, his eyes unbelieving.

"You're going to be fine," he said. "You're going to be fine." Papa did nothing but smile.

"No, I'm not," he took my hand into his, "and that's okay." I shook my head, the tears blurring my vision refusing to go away.

"No."

"It's okay." He squeezed my hand. "I'm so proud of you." He turned to my brother.

"Take care of each other."

Papa took off his leather-band watch and pressed it into Amrit's palm.

"I was going to give it to you when you graduated." He turned away, and I held onto his hand a little tighter as he coughed up the blood that had entered his lungs.

"I can't stop the bleeding," the medic mumbled angrily, but he didn't stop. He, like me, was clinging to whatever chance there was of recovery. He wanted to save the life of the man he had come to know as a brother.

"I can't do this without you," I choked out, reasoning with him as if he was leaving by a choice of his own.

"You already have."

I shook my head.

"I'll be lonely," I said.

"Take this." He took off the family ring, his wedding ring, and curled my fingers over it.

"Whenever you feel alone, hold onto it, and I'll be there."

"Hold on, man," said the medic as he started doing chest compressions. The woman standing by him, their leader, pushed his arms away.

"He's gone."

His hand went limp, and the light faded from his eyes. And just like that, he was gone. I would never hear him laugh again or see him smile. His empty body mirrored the hundreds that branded the estate.

Those words echoed in my ears as arms wrapped around me. This was a new pain. It wasn't physical. No, it was worse than that, far worse. It was like someone was tearing into my soul and ripping it into pieces. It hurt so much more than a wound, so much more than losing someone I had only known for a short time.

The medic closed my father's eyes before he left quietly. I sat there with my brother, his grief much more apparent than mine, and tried to let go. The sun was on the horizon when they came to take him away. I held onto Papa's arm to keep them from taking him, but Amrit grabbed his wrist before I could. I sat back, defeated, before he let go of me to give me the space that seemed foreign.

I had seen so much pain and death that I always thought the two were intertwined, but they weren't. This time, death was different. There was a sense of peace. It was the look in my father's eyes and the way he smiled carelessly like he used to when I was younger. He had no regrets. He had been ready to die, and to this day, I don't know why. Maybe it was because he knew that whatever came next would be better than this world or maybe, it was because he had lived, truly and boundlessly in a way that fulfilled him. Whatever it was, it surpassed the regret I often held with me after death. I would miss him, always, but there was nothing left unsaid, nothing undone. It was peaceful, and that was all that mattered.

The pulsing pain in my heart didn't stop with that belief, but my mind had calmed. I had found the resolve I searched for with every death, and it was enough. At least, that was what I had tried to convince myself.

The medic, Michael, came to me that evening with a few of my father's belongings. There was a photo with the corners tinted red and a small notebook he used as a diary. He wrote to us every day, and the photo, I ran my fingers over the worn material, it was the same one I kept in my room, the same one my mother kept in her purse. It was all that was left of my beautiful past.

"I'm sure they're in a better place," I said as my hands grazed the grass.

"They are."

"How do you know," I asked as my eyes lingered on the sky.

"I can feel it. They're finally free."

The world was calm. The birds chirped quietly, and the wind, ever so endless, flew through the grass and the leaves.

"Can we pray?" I asked, my voice rough and worn.

"Yeah." Amrit kept me close as I let my head fall and closed my tired eyes.

Please, take care of them.

Present Day

CHAPTER FORTY-ONE

The Others

It had been a week since the funeral, a week since I had freed Midnight and left that prison. It had been a week in this camp hidden as a recreation center. Beds lined the gym, many of them full but just barely. The people in them changed every day as the men and women here longer than me left, and those who had just arrived tried to make a temporary place for themselves.

A few buses came in the mornings with the newly liberated. I would always wait for them in the heat, hoping that one of them held family, while Amrit stayed in his hospital bed. He had slept a lot these past few days. I was supposed to sleep too, to recover, the doctor said, but it was fleeting, slipping out of my hands like dry sand. It never seemed to stay.

Another bus would come today. It was another chance to find someone, anyone, and it was my last chance. No more would come after this one.

The bus parked against the curb, and the door opened. One by one, people filed out in front of the building and lined up to go inside. I watched them carefully as I read their expressions and switched them for the ones I was more used to seeing. My doubt cleared with the last person, and finally, my hope had shrunk to nothing. No one had made it out alive. No one, not even Aunt Inaya, had survived to see the light of this day because no one else was here.

I went back to the area converted into a hospital ward. Amrit looked up from his place on the bed in his usual worry. He had been increasingly protective since the funeral, and despite my constant assurances, he never seemed to believe me when I told him that I was okay.

"Anyone?"

I shook my head, crestfallen.

"It's okay," he whispered.

I didn't believe him.

"I'll be with you tomorrow."

I ignored the pain in his eyes. "The doctor's letting you go?"

"I should be fine as long as I let myself heal properly. You know what that means," he said with a smile. It was an attempt to return to a normal that didn't have the constant reminder of people we had lost.

"I'm not carrying you," I said, quietly.

"Then I'm not leaving this bed."

I smiled. "I have an injured shoulder, remember."

"Right," he sighed. "I was really looking forward to it, though."

"You are so weird."

He frowned at me. "I carried you when you sprained your ankle."

"I was ten."

"Exactly! You owe me."

I turned away as my mind started to crave the solitude I had grown accustomed to this past week.

"I'm going out for a walk."

"I'll go with you." Amrit said as he tried to stand up, but I was too stuck in my own mind to notice him.

"I'll be back soon."

He sat down as I walked off, my hands stuffed in the hoodie given as a gift from the people who ran this place.

The building was straightforward, but it was easy to get lost when I didn't pay attention. I would go all the way to the other side, sometimes. It wasn't big, by any means, but I would often find myself alone in a shadowed hallway. I passed by countless rooms holding meetings or supplies or refugees before I slowed by the only room with a television in the entire building. It was always filled with children who usually watched whatever cartoons they could find. I joined them, sometimes, but today, there was something different on the screen. It was the revolutionaries' victory speech. I leaned on the doorframe and listened curiously.

"A country is only as righteous as the character of its people, and democracy, the passageway to freedom, is left in the hands of those able enough to call themselves American."

I smiled, amused. Thousands had died, hundreds were still enslaved, and the government was in pieces, but still, they were proud of the nation they called their own. I turned around and continued on my usual path, walking until I found myself in a hallway I had never been in before. Darkness reigned in the absence of the lights above and silence resonated from the empty and unused space. No one was supposed to be here, but, oddly enough, I wasn't alone.

"I need to go back." A woman shoved the other into the wall.

"Where? No one's looking for you." The woman took the stack of clothes the girl held onto and threw them to the floor.

"I should …"

"Your people did this!" She yelled as her hand wrapped around the girl's jaw.

"And now, you're going to pay." The two beside her held the girl back while the woman drove her fist into her abdomen.

I wanted to turn away. I wanted so badly to turn around and walk back, but I couldn't, and it was only because of one thing. I knew that if it had been just a few years ago instead of today, I would be in her place and she would be in mine. I didn't know if she would look away like the rest. I didn't even know if she deserved the kindness I so recklessly gave, but I would offer it, because I still believed in Ms. Garcia's perfect future. It was a hopeless thought, but one I had managed to hold onto.

"Let her go."

They did nothing but look over and snicker.

"Don't get involved in things that aren't about you, Terror, or I might just think that you two were friends."

I'm really going to regret this.

"Let her go," I repeated.

The woman's amusement disappeared the moment she moved forward. She lunged at me with her fist. I stepped away, and she stumbled forward, furious as she turned back to me. She tried to punch me again, but I grabbed her arm from the side and twisted it behind her back with ease. It was a trick I had learned from an old friend.

She tried to call to the others, but I pulled her arm up even higher. She cried out, and for a second, I hesitated. She ripped away and cradled her arm to her chest.

"Go," I said, my voice cold and firm.

They ran out and their footsteps continued to echo in the near empty hallway until they were long gone.

"Thank you." The girl said as she held the clothes close to her chest. I glanced at her but did nothing more as I turned around and walked away, though her deep green eyes were kind and somewhat familiar.

"W-Wait!" She ran forward and started walking beside me. "Can I join you?"

My hand went to my father's ring. I clenched it as it hung on the silver chain around my neck. I kept this part of him with me, even though it was a constant reminder that he was gone.

"No," I said. She faltered as I turned the corner. My mind was stuck in what seemed to be a permanent solitude, but I had no intention of moving out of it. It was the only consolation that gave me any type of relief.

I went to the main gym next. It was similar to my usual path, the same one I had taken to following this past week or so. There were groups of people lined up to get small bags packed with simple things like clothes and shoes. I didn't look at them. They were nothing more than a reminder of what I used to be.

A man shoved past me in a simple act of antipathy, and I staggered, if only for a moment.

It was a blessing, that second. Nothing less than a blessing.

I caught sight of a child. His hair was cut close to his scalp, and his skin was covered in dirt and small scars. His clothes were torn, but from the side, he looked familiar. It was a slight recognition, but it piqued my curiosity. I leaned forward, and when he turned away, I went to him. I touched his shoulder, and he jerked away before his eyes fell on me. A scar ran down the side of his face, and his left eye was dull. Latif blinked.

"Bhenji?"

I knelt down before my knees gave out and caught his embrace. He was so small in my arms and so fragile. His tears soaked into my injured shoulder as I held him.

"They hurt you," I whispered. "I'm so sorry."

"Don't hold up the line!" a man yelled.

I pulled away with a smile and stood with him as he got his things. His hand never left mine, and he leaned into me until we walked away.

He stopped as soon as we made it through the door and rubbed his arms nervously, until he raised them. I picked him up with my good arm and my eyes, my worn eyes, filled with tears again when he rested his head on my shoulder.

My brother was where I had left him, sitting silently.

"Amrit," I whispered. He nearly fell off the bed.

"Oh my God," He rushed to me as well as he could and put a hand on his brother's back.

Latif's grip on me grew until I pulled him away.

"Look over, buddy." His hand clutched onto my shirt in fear, but he did as I said. He started crying, and Amrit took him in his arms.

"Ali never came," he said. "Ammi said that he would save us, but he never came."

Amrit tried to cover up the pain in his expression.

"I'm sorry he's not here, but I won't let them hurt you anymore. I promise."

Latif pulled away and wiped away Amrit's tears.

"Don't cry," he said. Amrit wiped away what was left of his tears and nodded with a small smile.

"Okay." He sat him down and began telling him about how much he had grown.

The twitching in my hands grew by the passing seconds. They hurt him. God, he was still so young, so innocent. He didn't deserve this, but then again, none of us did.

I stayed with them for the remainder of the day, my impulse for solitude nearly gone, and soon enough, the sun had fallen. We left Amrit with a final goodbye and made the short journey to the beds we had claimed as ours.

It was quiet that night. A man's soft snores were the only sound that I could hear, and though a few others were whispering to each other, nothing clear reached my ears.

It was a lot like before, when we were too young to realize that we had to grow up, sooner or later, and before we had to learn how to take care of ourselves. It was a beautiful time, to revel in the innocent freedom of youth before time ripped it away. I yearned for something similar now, lying in the quiet darkness. I wanted to learn how to live again.

"Bhen?" a hushed voice asked.

"Yeah, buddy?"

"Are you awake?"

I stared up at the ceiling with my hands resting under my head. I hummed as Latif sat up.

"Can't sleep?" I asked. He shook his head and slid off his bed to sit on the edge of mine.

"Will you tell me a story?"

I moved over to make room for him.

"Which one?"

"A happy story," he said as he curled up next to me. I let my mind wander for a few seconds before I remembered my favorite bedtime stories. They were filled with warriors and kingdoms. It was my history, and the very basis of my legacy, so I told them to him the way my father used to tell them to me. I smiled when he did and suppressed a laugh when he giggled beside me. I created a different world so that he could forget his, even if it was just for a little while, and stopped talking only when his breathing had evened.

It was a simple kindness, a small deed, but more often than not, it was the type of thing that would stay with him over the years, just as it had stayed with me.

In the End

CHAPTER FORTY-TWO

A Time to Heal

I stood by the road and stared up at the sky. This was it, I suppose, the end of the story that would define the rest of my life. It was my story. Some would see it as something to be celebrated. *You made it!* Others would pity the circumstances of my life, and few would share my pain. There was only so much people could understand, only so much they were willing to imagine, but it was all there in the depths of my soul. I would hide the grief and move on until I learned to live with the scars that clung to me like a shadow.

I have learned many things in my life, but two hold importance still. The first is simple. People cannot be defined by something as simple and translucent as color or religion or bloodline. The complexity of life doesn't allow for such a thing. The second is not as uncomplicated. It is the value of a smile, of laughter, true and pure, and the beautiful innocence of happiness. Some will understand this, as I have come to, but others will not. As is the way of the world.

"Where to now?" Amrit asked.

The war had been fought and won. My heart was still pounding in my chest with certain regularity. I often wondered how it could, with all its permanent scars and bruises. They would heal with time, as all things did, but the memories would remain. The forgotten hopes and dreams, the people I had left behind, all of it would never leave me.

"Wherever the wind takes us."

As had been the uncertainty of my life. With nowhere for us to go and nothing but the clothes on our backs, there was no clear direction. There was nothing left for us here, no family and no name aside from the one we could make for ourselves. Everything was gone. It was surreal, that moment. It felt like only yesterday that I was coming home from the library with a stack of books in my arms. A part of me still believed that my family was waiting for me at the dinner table, ready to eat when I arrived.

"No, really." His voice was distant. "What do we do now?" It was the only question I had no real answer to.

"I don't know."

The End

About the Author

Ekjoatroop Kaur is a Sikh American writer based out of Kansas, and has been writing for nearly a decade. She is currently a student at the University of Missouri-Kansas City majoring in biology and chemistry on the pre-med track. As a SikhLEAD internship alum, she is very involved in her Sikh community.

In her spare time, she teaches Gatka to the Sikh youth and practices Kirtan with her family. She also works with Nishkam TV as the head scriptwriter for a contemporary project and is the Kansas Representative of the North American Sikh Medical and Dental Association (NASMDA).

Ekjoatroop was a panelist for the 2021 Parliament of World Religions speaking on Sikhi and Solidarity and she is the co-founder of Sikhs of Today and Tomorrow.

For the Sake of It is Ekjoatroop Kaur's debut novel and she hopes to promote conversation and discussion over a number of current issues with her book.